# Forgiving Waters

Kenneth L. Capps

Published in the United States by BQB Publishing
(Boutique of Quality Books Publishing Company)
www.bqbpublishing.com

Printed in the United States of America

978-1-937084-55-4 (p)
978-1-937084-67-7 (h)
978-1-937084-56-1 (e)

Library of Congress Control Number: 2012936182

Book design by Robin Krauss, www.lindendesign.biz

# 1

All day and into the evening, the Texas skies over the Gulf of Mexico brewed like a witch's cauldron, sucking up moisture from the abundant waters of the Gulf. A cleansing rain made its approach in the calm of darkness, a calm soon upended by a spectacular display of nature's fury against the pitch sky. For Beauregard "Bo" Lee Kelso, the storm had already infected his dreams, changing them to nightmares—the same nightmares that had haunted him, in one way or another, for years. He did not wake when the thunder roared or the lightning pierced the land, the brilliance invading every small line in the shutters and shades of his Texas ranch house. He slept fitfully, tormented by his past, distraught for his future.

*"No! Pa, please!" the little boy's voice cried out from Bo's nightmare.*

*"Shut your mouth, boy, and hold the shotgun on him!"—the voice of his father erupts in the turbulent moment.*

*Then, his mother's plea: "Leroy, let him go! You can't do this. You know who he is! Just have the law take care of it!"*

*"You shut your mouth, Annabel, and get in the house!" Annabel ran to the house but did not enter. Instead she turned as she reached the top steps of their porch and continued to plead with her husband not to hang the man who'd been caught leaving their house, apparently a robbery thwarted. Her high-pitched tone of panic was amplified, as she repeatedly screamed, "You can't do this. Let him go!"*

"No, Pa! Please no!" Bo cried aloud through his tormented dream. However, now seventy-three years since that scene had passed for real, there was no one to hear him, no one to rescue him. Not the horses sleeping in the barn. Not the mockingbird resting in the fig tree outside his window. His wife, in death, may have heard him, but she could not help him. He was alone, frantic in the darkness of his dream state, unable to detach himself from it, the terror punctuated in a stage set of thunder and lightning.

*"You take a good look at this, boy. This is what a thief looks like. A low-down, worthless colored," Leroy Kelso spat, disdain and pure anger consuming his leathered face. "You give him a job, and this is what he does. He is nothing but a low-down thief, and this is what you do with a thief. Now you hold that shotgun on him, boy," the old man said as he moved quickly toward a horse buggy parked next to the house and retrieved a section of rope.*

*The boy whimpered as his thin body shook at the sheer horror of the scene unfolding before him. "Please, Pa, don't do this!" But his words fell unheeded to the grass underfoot.*

*His mother's voice was relentless in its plea for reason and restraint. "Leroy, you can't do this."*

*"The hell I can't! No colored is going to break into my house and steal from me and get away with it."*

*The sedan headlights tore through the storm of the boy's terror, highlighting the waxy shine of damp skin on this black man he had known all his life. The weight of the shotgun was enormous for Bo's eleven-year-old frame. He could barely keep it raised, much less level. The barrel was so long it could almost touch the shaking knees of Calvin Mercer, who kneeled on the ground, crying shamelessly, doing his own fair share of begging for Leroy Kelso not to hang him.*

*"Please, Mr. Kelso, let me go, and I'll never come back here again. I swear it; I'll leave town. You'll never see me again. Jus' don't hang me, please! My family . . ."*

*"Shut. Your. Mouth!" Leroy's voice rivalled thunder.*

*Annabel pleaded: "Let him go, Leroy. This ain't right . . . you know it ain't right."*

*Unabashedly desperate, Calvin tried to bargain with Leroy*

*Kelso to spare him. But Leroy Kelso, in his own world of hate and intolerance, blinked not an eye nor listened. He stepped back and threw the rope over one of the low-hanging limbs of a pin oak tree that reached its massive branches across the majority of the front yard. Its roots crawled along the ground throughout the entire circumference of the tree, rising up like gravestones.*

*"Get up, you worthless thief."*

*Calvin could not move; he was petrified with fear. Kelso would not be deterred. He quickly fashioned the end of the rope into a noose and flung it around the sobbing man's neck as he said, "Fine, I'll just hoist you up to your feet."*

*In a snap of realization, Calvin raised his hands to his neck, grabbing the noose as Kelso tightened it. His scarred, dark fingers wrapped around the hemp rope as it bit into his flesh, like tiny razors on his neck and hands.*

*The sound of Calvin's sobbing permeated Bo's young soul. He was learning for the first time in his life the true meaning of the word fear and the preamble to suffering.*

*Bo' s father towered over Calvin as he struggled, half-slumped and half-kneeling at the rancher's feet.*

*Somewhere between Calvin's writhing pleas for mercy and Mrs. Kelso's screams for reason, young Bo Kelso dropped the shotgun. It fell to the ground and bounced off one of the oak roots protruding out of the ground. Both hammers on the old double-barreled Browning slammed down and it went off.*

*Like thunder.*

Bo awoke from his torment as an enormous clap of thunder erupted outside his window. He sat up and swung both his weary legs over the side of the bed, feet hitting the hardwood floor, and grasped his hair firmly as he held his head with both hands.

"I had that dream again, Mary Beth. You know the one, where Pa was going to hang Calvin." For just a second, he thought he heard his loving wife whisper, "It's okay, honey. It's long past." Dead now three years, Mary Beth would be at best a ghost. Nonetheless, he was comforted. As he turned his sleepy gaze toward her side of the bed, the lightning flashed, shining a spotlight on the bedding that used to be filled with the preciousness of his wife. In that snap of illumination, he saw the comforter untouched on her pillow, neatly folded, undisturbed.

The clock on the nightstand read three thirty. Unable to sleep, he felt around in the dark for his slippers. He found one, put it on his foot, and then probed around with his toes for the other. When he placed it on his foot, it felt strange. He reached down and removed it with his hand. It was Mary Beth's slipper. He kept them just under the edge of the bed next to his, one of many nods to his devotion to her memory. This comforted him, easing the echo of loss that he would never shake. "It's okay, honey. It's long past." This time, he acknowledged her message with an indiscernible smile.

# 2

Bo Kelso lived alone on the land his family had mastered for generations. His two sons, both attorneys and unresolved to the life of a rancher, lived in downtown Houston with their families, a little more than fourteen miles away. Bo loved his sons, respected their choices, and encouraged them fully; it was what Mary Beth had wanted for them and something he'd never had as a child: a choice.

Though much of the land had been sold off to the leanings of forward progress, the remaining Kelso property of five hundred acres was a grand paradise of ancient trees and lush vegetation dotting the fragrant green pastures. Several ponds, along with the shallow waters of Clear Creek, fed the thirsty fields and cattle. Back in the late 1800s, after the Civil War, thousands of cattle grazed here when Bo's grandfather had purchased Kelso Ranch. The livestock had since dwindled to just a few Angus cattle, some goats, and twelve horses that were more like pets than anything else. A handful of ranch hands and contract labor helped maintain the property.

Upon a horse of the richest chestnut, uncut by other colors, Bo surveyed the vast land daily, checking the fences and livestock. Whisky by the Drink, a retired champion Texas cutting horse, was a devoted friend to Bo. There were times the old man would swear the horse could read his mind.

In the predawn morning, Bo avoided turning on the lights in the ranch house, knowing it would just incite the morning-hungries in the horses in the barn, including Whisky. For them, the sign of first light meant that food would soon be coming.

He marveled at how the fairly commonplace, rambunctious thunderstorms blowing in from the Gulf of Mexico did not disturb the livestock, but a light in his kitchen window could cause them to stir, letting you know of their expectations sometimes in not so quiet ways.

In the darkness of the bedroom, Bo found his glasses and picked up the small journal off his desk—a journal that he always carried with him. He walked silently into the parlor, which was situated in the front of the house and facing away from the barn. His worn leather chair made a welcoming sound as it stretched under his weight. He flipped on a small reading light that hung over his left shoulder, opened up the brown leather book, and began to write to his wife, as he had done so many times in the past three years.

My Dearest Mary Beth,

I write to you with a heavy heart and a crippling pain in my soul. I talk to you every day, and I know you hear me because the mockingbird still sings and the flowers bloom with colors as brilliant as your smile. Whisky and I ride every day and keep each other company. He still looks over my shoulder every morning as I brush his back and saddle him. He searches for your face in the windows and doorways of our home, hoping to see you. I feel as if he misses you as much as I do. I am able to soothe his grieving with half of an apple, taking his mind off wondering where you have gone. I wish there were such an apple for me. I would join you right now if God would allow it. I know it is the only thing that would soothe my relentless sorrow. Still, as much as I long for this, there are things I still must do before I can truly join you in peace.

My darling, I have held this inside me for about a year now, though surely you've known the truth anyway. For many years, I held firmly to the belief that an innocent man was guilty, accusing him of something that he did not do. An honest man, he has done me no harm. I have caused him great pain and loss through my own arrogance and prejudice, of which I thought I held none. So heavy is this burden on me, Mary Beth, that I fear God will not hear my prayers for forgiveness. I write to you and beg you, please carry my words to His ears, for it is my sin that I fear will keep me from joining you in heaven.

Bo closed his book and neatly tucked the pen away between the last two pages. He removed his reading glasses and slowly brought the side of his calloused hand back to his eye to catch a rogue tear. He closed his eyes and fell to sleep.

He was soon greeted by the lingering dream, so often his subconscious companion, but more so in the past year. The discovery of that tractor, the one that had disappeared in 1942, must have conjured up the ugly memories of his past. And there he was again, a frightened eleven-year-old boy, caught up in the world of unjust accusations and a father's contempt.

# 3

"Damn you, boy, you could have killed both of us!" his father bellowed, reaching down and picking up the shotgun, both barrels still spewing smoke.

In that moment, Calvin saw an opportunity and seized it. Throwing the noose from his neck, he ran as if a world-class sprinter. Any terror he'd previously shown was gone, or at least irrelevant, for this race. Perhaps the sound of that shotgun held healing qualities, allowing him to run as he did. Before Leroy could reach into the sedan and reload the shotgun, Calvin had disappeared into the darkness, crashing through the thicket— possibly on his way home, more likely to some safer, other place.

The shotgun blast had alerted the half-dozen or so cowboys sleeping in the bunkhouse about a hundred yards away. The first to arrive at the front yard was a sleepy-eyed cowboy named Harrigan. His hair was twisted in knots—what was not matted down was sticking up and pointing in every direction. He had on a pair of overalls that he held up by the waist. Upon seeing him, Leroy ordered him to wake up the rest of the boys and saddle the horses. He wanted them to follow his sedan down the road as he chased after Calvin. Harrigan made his barefoot sprint back to the bunkhouse, shouting out to the others to saddle up.

Bo's father then turned to him and grabbed him by the collar, dragging him along as he stretched out his steps in long strides to the sedan. Bo's feet lifted from the ground; only his toes skipped along the dirt as his shirt bunched up into both his armpits, as if it were a harness.

"You're coming with me, boy. You're going to help me find that thieving colored, and when we do, I'm going to hang him on the nearest tree I can find."

Bo sobbed uncontrollably as he sat in the front seat of the sedan, while his father retrieved the rope from over the limb. Leroy rolled it up around his thick arm.

Bo's mom was heading toward the sedan. "Let him go, Leroy," she said, in a final attempt to stop the one-track train that was her husband.

"Get back in the house like I told you, Annabel. This is none of your concern."

He jumped into the black Ford sedan, headlights piercing the darkness, as he drove like a lunatic across the bridge, behind the barn, and through the woods. The dirt road on the other side of the bridge led to their pasture, which eventually joined Clover Town—the pasture that Calvin would have to cross, hundreds of acres wide and as many deep. The grass was ankle-high and shimmered under the late-evening full moon, which shined brightly over the vast patch of pure green. If Calvin had crossed the pasture, he would easily be seen.

His father was ranting, and the intensity of his anger frightened Bo. The youngster could not control himself and cried.

"That's enough of that, boy!" his father yelled as he reached out and shook Bo several times before letting go and slapping his own thigh loudly. "Be a man! This is what men do to protect their property. A thief ain't any good to anyone. Especially colored thieves."

Bo immediately stopped crying; his father had never put his hands on him before. Usually when he was angry, he would use his powerful voice, the same voice he used to scream at cowboys and ranch hands across the pastures. Whenever Bo heard that tone in his father's voice, Bo understood he'd reached the limits of his patience. Still, the worst thing his father had ever done was make him walk home without his horse as punishment for upsetting him while out working the livestock. He never laid a hand on him. Until now.

When his father latched onto him with his massive hand, his fingers drove into his flesh and Bo could feel the physical power of his anger. Bo suddenly had a sense, probably just a fraction, of Calvin's terror.

All the cowboys from the bunkhouse met up with the sedan after a short time, telling Leroy that they had seen nothing between the thicket and the pasture. They surmised the accused had gotten into Clear Creek and made his way off the property.

Father and son drove back to the ranch house. As they emerged from the thicket, their lights illuminated someone walking on the road, not far from where Calvin had fallen when he'd tripped trying to escape these same lights a short time ago. This time, it was Annabel, carrying a burlap feed sack in her arms. When she saw the lights of the sedan coming up the road, she stopped and turned to face them. Leroy slowed the sedan and hollered out the window, "What in tarnation are you doing out here, woman?"

She walked over to the door and threw the sack into her husband's lap.

"Take a good look at this and tell me what you see," she said, spitting the words through tears and red anger. She screamed, "Tell me what you see, Leroy?"

"Where did you get this?" Leroy asked as he fumbled through the sack of canned goods, a wrapped ham, and other food items.

"This is what Calvin was stealing. Food! Leroy, it's food from our kitchen. You should be ashamed of yourself. If you've ever in your life been ashamed of yourself, you should be ashamed right now."

"What are you talking about, Annabel?"

"You're just like your father, cruel and insensitive. A man who steals food from your kitchen is desperate, not a thief." With that, she turned in disgust and headed back to the house.

"Annabel!" Leroy shouted after her as she walked into the darkness toward the porch light. She did not respond, her body language clear as she swung her arms and marched with her back straight, shoulders squared. Bo and Leroy had both seen that walk before. Annabel was serious, and it wouldn't be easy to stop her from getting what she wanted.

Leroy drove past her and stopped the car in front of the house. When he opened the door, Annabel was approaching the porch, only a few feet away.

"Boy, get up to your room," he ordered.

———•———

Bo sprung from the car and into the house, making a beeline for his bedroom. His window was above the front porch, and he could hear every word his parents said, even as they tried to speak in low voices.

"That man didn't come here to steal from us; he came here to ensure the survival of his family," his mom said. "There is no worse pain than being hungry, and for a father of two, there's no worse pain than seeing your family go hungry."

Bo heard the screen door creak open, but didn't hear it slam shut.

"Let go of my arm now, Annabel. It's time to get to bed. We'll talk more about this in the morning."

"No, we'll talk about it right now. You pay your colored hands next to nothing for their backbreaking labor. They walk here to work every day, and they have been loyal to your family for years. They live in squalor with nothing, but they make do and show up here to work on time every day; some of them in their bare feet! And you sure can't say the same about that bunkhouse full of drunken cowboys yonder. They can't wake up on time to get to work, and they're less than a hundred feet from the barn! When they do finally wake up, the coloreds are already here working. They are the ones that made this ranch what it is. You know as well as I do that it's their sweat and muscle and loyalty that made you and your father rich." Her voice was full tilt now. Mom was on a roll. "And if it weren't for Mammy Dupree, you wouldn't be walking this earth, Leroy Kelso. She wet-nursed you when your mother died of the fever six months after you were born. You owe your life and livelihood to people like Calvin. You have forgotten that."

Bo stepped back from the window, momentarily stunned by this bit of history he'd not before known.

———•———

Back on the porch, having quietly closed the screen door, Leroy sat down on one of the benches on the front porch. He stared out into the darkness and quietly contemplated his wife's words; all true. Still, he felt no remorse in his heart, only a sense of duty he felt entitled to enforce and a frustration with his inability to argue his wife's point.

"Calvin would have never done this unless he was desperate," Annabel continued. "And you want to hang him for being hungry, a hunger that you created because you are a bigot!"

"It ain't like that, Annabel. I pay that man," he reminded. "He gets an honest wage. If he needed more money, he should have asked me for it instead of stealing from me. He probably had somebody else with him that we didn't see, and he made it off into the woods. Calvin was probably just the last man out of the house and got caught."

"You're a fool, Leroy. Don't matter who it was or how many, this involves family—children—being hungry. Now I haven't checked the house yet, but I'm sure nothing is missing except your heart. You're not just a bigot; you're cruel, and you treat the colored labor like slaves."

The word touched a nerve. "Don't you ever use that word

here again! Slaves have never been on this property. My father and I have always paid freed coloreds to work this land."

Annabel turned her back on him and made her way into the house without another word. She let go of the screen door and it slammed shut behind her.

Leroy paced to the far end of the porch and sat down on the edge of a rocking chair. His hands were shaking in visible anger at what had transpired.

He chewed the side of his cheek—a nervous habit formed years ago—and considered all that happened: the betrayal of an employee, the lack of spine in his only son, and the fact that his own wife took the side of the thief. Sure, everything she'd said was true. His daddy had taught him everything he needed to know about running a ranch and being successful. But he'd taught him nothing about compassion. His mother had not been there to nurture that foreign emotion in her son's heart. His brother and sister had both died at young ages due to illness. Life on the ranch had been extremely difficult, especially for the only child left to follow in the footsteps of a heartless, hard man. Still, he wasn't one to whine about his lot in life.

Mammy Dupree had essentially been his mother. A round, brilliantly dark woman, she'd nursed him to health and adulthood. As a baby, Leroy had slept in a small wooden crib propped up on the far side of the kitchen during the cold winters and in the same crib on the back porch during the summer. The first day he crawled from the crib on his own signaled the end of his childhood. From that moment on, his father carried him on horseback or wagon everywhere he went in the fields. Leroy never had the opportunity to play with the other children; they were colored and he was the son of a rancher who knew nothing but work.

Leroy could only hear his own learned hatred and entitlement drumming in his ears. His daddy had always been a whole lot more worried about himself and his ranch than about helping others. Compassion had not been a factor in any of his thoughts or actions. He'd treated people poorly in general, whether black or white, only seeing them as a means to an end. But the black hands definitely had been treated worst of all, animals included. And Leroy carried that ranching legacy with him to this very moment.

He sat in the darkness of the porch long enough to convince himself that the entire situation was misunderstood by Annabel and that his way was the best way.

<hr />

In his room, leaning far away from the side of the window, to see but not be seen, Bo held his breath so as not to move even the air. He watched his father walk from the porch to the small, wooden garage-like structure next to the house where the sedan was kept. Through the blur of the window screen, Bo could make out his father's silhouette as he entered the building and emerged from it with a bottle of what Bo knew was whisky, his father's drink of choice. He put the bottle to his lips and turned it up. The whisky bottle glistened under the glare of the moon. His father took a pull and started walking, as if into the moonlight, finally sitting down on a tree stump. He rolled a cigarette and lit it, the red embers illuminating his face each time he took a drag. Occasionally he would sip from the bottle, and then return it to its perch next to him on the stump.

Bo had seen this routine before; his father usually drank alone, like tonight. The ritual seemed to soothe his father. After a short while and another cigarette, he returned the whisky bottle to its hiding place and headed to the house, grinding his last cigarette in the dirt at the foot of the steps. He stepped inside the house. Bo heard not another word.

<hr />

The following morning the local sheriff was informed of what happened. Calvin Mercer was nowhere to be found. He'd made good on his promise to the rancher who'd wanted to hang him.

He vanished, leaving behind his young wife and two children. A short time after that, his wife and children also disappeared from Clover Town. Everyone assumed that the whole family moved far enough away so that no one could find them, especially Leroy Kelso.

# 4

The morning light found Bo still sleeping in his leather chair. He stood, made his way into the kitchen, and turned on the coffeepot. He was usually up by six fifteen, admiring the sunlight as it began its glow through the tree line just beyond the barn, the orange and red slowly expanding into brighter and brighter yellow and gold. By now, he would have had his shower and a second cup of coffee, and would be about to walk out the back door, down the porch, and across the strip of grass that led to the barn. There he would saddle Whisky by the Drink and make his morning rounds of the property. However, on this particular morning, everything was out of sorts, and he was late. For the first time since Mary Beth's passing, he broke his routine—but not by design.

From the kitchen window over the sink, Bo could see that the barn light was on. Clint's truck was parked on the left-hand side of the hitching post.

Clint worked for Bo's oldest son Clay. He was paid by the family estate, set up by the Kelso boys when the family had sold the majority of the ranch property so Bo could retire. Clint was in his late forties with gray hair and bursts of tight wrinkles around his pale-blue eyes. Tall and wiry, he stood six foot two and weighed just over one hundred seventy pounds. Bo was sure that Clint would blow away in a strong Texas breeze. The job seemed to suit Clint to a tee, though, and he was as reliable as the rising of the sun.

Waiting for the coffee to finish its brew, he looked again out the window, soaking in the inherent beauty of the dawning day.

He noticed Clint now just inside the barn, staring intently at the large chalkboard nailed to the wall by the tack room, reading the chore list for any given day. Clint always had a cowboy hat on his head—sometimes black and sometimes brown—but always a cowboy hat. The only time Bo ever saw him take it off his head was when he read the chores written on the chalkboard, and at those times, he would massage his fingers through his gray hair as he contemplated the day's work. In his usual wobbly gait, caused by a bum knee from rodeo days gone by and bulldogging steers, Clint worked until noon seven days a week. The remainder of each day was his own.

The smell of freshly brewed coffee cleared the cobwebs from Bo's head. He poured himself a bit, caressing the cup as he lifted it to his lips.

"It doesn't taste the same," he said aloud. "Three years of trying and I still can't make it taste the way you made it, Mary Beth. I am using the same coffee, the same coffeemaker, everything, and it doesn't taste the same." In a dramatic, beseeching tone, he looked upward: "Please tell me, honey. What am I doing wrong?"

His words dangled in the air, unanswered.

He finished a second cup of coffee as he listened to an early-morning talk show on the radio. He left it on as he showered, shaved, and then dressed. It was now almost seven o'clock as he turned off the radio, exited the house, and locked the door behind him. He started his walk to the barn with some trepidation. This was the beginning of a day he had been dreading.

He was on his way to the neighborhood on the far backside of his property to speak to Samuel Clover, the preacher of the Clover Town Pentecostal Church—the church attended by Elijah Waters and his family, the church that had helped raise the money for Elijah's attorney. Bo had spoken to Pastor Clover by phone the day before and arranged to meet on that morning.

The warm colors of a rising sun peeped through the tree line on the other side of Clear Creek. Bo stopped a few hundred feet short of his barn to take it all in. There was no wind, and the stillness was hypnotic.

"Thank you, God, for this day," he said in a low voice. A short prayer—it was one he repeated often.

He stood there long enough to see the sun creep above the roofline of the barn, flooding the horizon with the richness of morning. As if on cue, an orchestra of songbirds began their morning serenade to all who would listen.

Bo bowed his head in deference to the moment. *Surely,* he thought, *this is the best time of the day for an old cowboy like me.*

As he entered the barn, he was almost run over by Clint, who strolled past with a wheelbarrow full of feed almost overflowing its edges. He also balanced a five-gallon bucket and a small shovel on top of the feed, stopping at each stall along the west wall of the barn. The twelve horses, six on the west side and six on the east side, poked their heads out over the stall doors. They anxiously awaited their breakfast. Some whinnied, others stomped their hooves, while others rattled their stall doors.

"I see you got your hands full this morning," Bo said as he passed Clint on his way to Whisky's stall.

"Yep, like always." Clint replied.

Then he asked, "The boy?" referring to Matt, a nineteen-year-old hand who had just started working at the ranch three months earlier and had not made it into work on time yet.

"Sooner or later he might show up. We could use some reliable help around here," Clint replied as he entered one of the stalls to feed Stopper. Stopper's full name was Showstopper because of his muscular lines and tall stance. One of the finest cutting horses in Texas, he could outmaneuver any calf and slice through a herd like a needle pulling through cotton.

With the birds singing, the sun rising, and the animals demanding breakfast, the sounds and sights of the morning were a live symphony to a cowboy. Conversation was unnecessary—

everything that needed saying was on the chalkboard or could wait.

Bo walked to the end of the barn to Whisky's stall. Nailed above his stall was an oak board, upon which *Whisky by the Drink* was meticulously carved. Underneath the horse's name was the horse's birthday, April 17, 1969. It was a special day to Bo, and for more personal reasons too. Each horse in the barn had the same introduction nailed above each stall.

Unlike the other horses, Whisky was transfixed on the back of the house, where Mary Beth had so often made an appearance at this time of day. *Three years now and this magnificent horse is faithful to her memory*, Bo thought. It was a source of great pride to him, that his horse was so loyal and heart-driven. After all, if not for Mary Beth, man and beast may have never been united. *Another reason to love that woman.* Bo reached inside his jacket pocket and produced an apple, which glistened red, reflecting the overhead lights. He removed his pocketknife, opened it, and halved the apple. He now had Whisky's full attention.

"Good morning, old friend. Here. You may as well have it all since we're not riding today." He gave Whisky one half and then the other, then moved away from the stall so Clint could feed him.

"I don't need his tack out this morning, Clint," Bo said. "I'm going over to Clover Town to see someone. I should be back after lunch, so shut the house gate for me please."

"Figured," Clint responded. He followed up with, "Got on your best boots, fancy white shirt, and your best buckle on your belt. Figured."

"Yeah, can't get much by you," Bo said as he walked out the back of the barn toward his truck.

At the sound of the unmistakable crunch of gravel, Bo looked up. A young man had just pulled up to the front of the barn and jumped from his truck. He ran into the barn as if he were finishing a race.

"Sorry I'm late, Mr. Kelso!" he shouted as he passed, ranting all the while about the reasons and circumstances and why-fors and whatnots that kept him from being on time.

Bo nodded and replied with great earnestness, "You don't say," but kept walking toward his truck.

With Matt's arrival, the serenity of the morning was irreparably broken. Bo knew from experience that it would take awhile for a young wannabe cowboy like Matt to learn two of the most important cowboy lessons of all. First was how to gain the most from a conversation by using as few words as possible. And the second lesson was that early mornings should be allowed to wake up easy.

# 5

"Well, look at here. Good morning, Beauregard. It has been a while. A long while indeed." Reverend Samuel Clover clapped his hands once in punctuation of this greeting. He held his arms wide as Bo stepped from the truck.

Bo nodded with a tip of his hat, allowing the reverend to extend an arm across his back as he sought safe footing in the heavily pot-holed, oyster-shell lot. "Morning, Pastor."

The meeting Bo had stewed about with no small degree of anxiety was about to take place.

———•———

There had always been a Pastor Clover at the Clover Town Pentecostal Church. Samuel was the latest to lead the congregation. His father, and his father before him, had stood watch over the flock of believers ever since the first boards were laid and the first walls raised.

The church had been erected back in 1880. There was one long, open building, twenty-five feet wide and fifty feet long. When it was rebuilt in the spring of 1960, the church also doubled as a schoolhouse for the black community, a function of necessity to educate them at the time. If it hadn't been for the church building, the Clover young would have had a hard time accessing the benefits of schooling. The dirt roads leading to Clover Town had never been paved, making it difficult for the county buses to reach Clover. In the late '50s, the Houston Independent School District informed the residents that their children would have to meet at the end of the road that joined the paved main road in order to catch the bus.

That was a long two-mile walk for the kids to make twice a day—a walk in the mud on rainy days and a walk in the Texas sun all summer. The community decided it made more sense to start its own school, using the church for its humble beginnings. There were box fans in open windows for cooling, one heater stove for warmth, and a well of fresh water that was cool and sweet to the thirsty tongue. Two outhouses, now abandoned with their doors dangling precariously on one hinge, backed up to the fence which bordered the Kelso Ranch pasture.

In 1966, an anonymous donor sent a team of workers to install a septic system and bathrooms for the building. Though no one would ever come to know who this person was, the community showed its boundless appreciation by being the best of hosts to the workers. Each morning there was a table set up with fresh coffee, homemade pastries, scrambled eggs, and ham. And in the afternoons, the tables were as full as a Thanksgiving dinner, covered with fried chicken, turnip greens, boiled eggs, and the occasional fried catfish.

Things changed again for the community when the roads were paved in 1972, and the Clover Town children could attend school in Houston. The church then turned the buildings into a daycare and preschool for Clover Town's swelling population. But the building and its additions were showing their age. Paint, from years of repainting the outside walls, flaked off like the bottom of a dry lakebed. Boards buckled and bowed under the constant stress from the blazing Texas sun and the relentless beating from spring thunderstorms. Even the hardy cedar shake shingles, so carefully installed, were starting to abandon their positions and slide off the steeple roof, exposing small voids where black tar paper showed through.

———•———

Bo didn't notice the structural disrepair on that morning as he carefully navigated the overly moist parking lot filled with craters of muddy water courtesy of the previous night's storm. With the pastor at his elbow, he succeeded most of the time, though barely avoided several small craters that longed to eat his boots. It wasn't until he'd reached the grassy haven of the church lawn that he thought about the funding, or lack thereof, that would determine this precious landmark's future.

"Beauregard Lee Kelso!" Pastor Clover hollered with a grin, the unmistakable ring of friendship in his tone. "I declare, if'n I was a youngster, I'd pick that handle for myself. A fine southern name. It has a style about it, a certain *flair*." He said the word in fancified syllables: *flay-yah*. "I suppose you might call it southern royalty, don't you think so? Now what on earth brings you out here, Beauregard?"

Bo chuckled as he realized the truth to the adage: the more things change, the more they stay the same. Pastor Clover always went on that way; he was a preacher after all. He loved to hear himself talk. Any minute, Bo expected the preacher to ask him when was the last time he'd warmed up a pew with his backside.

Pastor Clover walked him over to the wooden fence that surrounded the playground. Each board was six inches wide and four feet high, several broken or loose, probably from a steady beating from kickballs and general antics of the youth. In less than two hours, the hordes of screaming children, freed from the confines of their preschool classroom, would spill onto the freshly mowed grass, which the pastor had worked on just after sun-up that morning.

"Lord, it sure would be nice to replace this old, rickety board fence with one made of chain-link. I think it might go a little longer in between repairs. What do you think, Beauregard?" Pastor Clover asked as he reached into his pocket and retrieved a brown handkerchief. He wiped his brow, which was coated in tiny beads of sweat.

"I reckon," Bo replied.

"Yes sir, a chain-link fence would be put to good use around here."

Bo knew Pastor Clover was driving home a point. He tried to let the conversation drift away, but the church leader would not be swayed otherwise.

"Say one about six feet high instead of four—that way, it would cut down on all the balls and toys I constantly have to fetch out of your cow pasture."

"I reckon," Bo replied once again.

"I hear that plastic balls, Frisbees, and other sorts of toys can be some kind of rough on a cow's digestive system."

"Yeah, I reckon that could be."

"Uh-huh," Clover quietly said as he put away his handkerchief and leaned back onto a newly repaired portion of the fence. "So, back to what I was saying."

"What was that? You mean the fence?"

"No. I mean what brings you out this way in your truck, dressed in your good clothes? It can't be to check the pasture or your fence 'cause you do that on Whisky, so it must be something special," Clover remarked.

There was a lengthy pause as Bo walked toward the pasture fence a few steps away. He felt uncomfortable. He stared at the distant tree line, as if the trees would help him with his words. What he'd wanted was to ask the pastor where he could find Elijah Waters, but the guilt he harbored only choked his words in his throat. The pause continued, the pastor patient.

Bo had finally gathered his thoughts and started to turn and face Clover, just as the brown-faced preacher man blurted out, "Oh, blessed Lord Jesus, I know what this is all about. Yes, of course! Beauregard Lee, you're here to give your soul to the Lord."

Shocked, Bo's mouth hung open. He protested, "No, I—"

Clover cut him off again. "Thank you, Lord Jesus. I have been praying for you all these years." He was in full Pentecostal preaching rant. "Tell me how it happened, brother. Did the good Lord come to you in a dream? Did you wake up speaking in tongues? Has the Holy Ghost got hold of you?" He then stomped his feet and spun around, clapping and raising his hands over his head, which he threw back in a joyous burst of laughter, dancing around on the healthy grass. "Lord, it's the little things that make an old country preacher like me so happy!"

"No! Now stop that, Samuel, that ain't it at all. Besides all that, I am Baptist! Baptists don't suddenly convert to being Pentecostal; it's the other way around. And stop calling me Beauregard! My mother is the only person that calls me that!"

Pastor Clover stopped his dancing and shouting and turned toward the schoolyard fence. Reaching out his arms, he grasped the top railing and leaned forward, facing away from Bo, trying to hide the swelling laughter that was building inside him.

Bo, completely perplexed, shouted, "That's not why I'm here!"

Pastor Clover turned around to face Bo with a smile so wide it hit both sides of his face. His eyes were mere thin slits, through which he peeped at Bo, who was doing all he could to control himself as realization took hold and the humor bubbled within him. It was no use.

Pastor Clover broke into laughter so loud that Bo was immediately infected by it. They hooted buoyantly, slapping knees and fences and hands. Each of their faces turned its own unique shade of red. Bo was surprised at himself for his lack of restraint. *It's wonderful,* he thought. He couldn't remember the last time he'd been so struck by comedy.

"You should have seen the look on your face, Beauregard; I thought you were going to jump the barbed wire fence and run."

"I thought that's what I'd have to do before you dragged me down to the creek for another baptism."

Their laughter started up again. Intermingled with the sound of their own voices were the muffled voices of children also laughing hysterically in unison. Clover and Bo turned toward the schoolhouse to witness all eight windows crowded with tiny black faces. Eyes and mouths open wide, they laughed without needing to know the punch line. They were looking at it! Their teachers beamed like children themselves, caught up in the hilarity of watching two grown men letting go of their inhibitions in a fit of merriment.

Upon noticing their audience, Clover and Bo joined arms and held onto each other's shoulders, moving away from the fence toward the parking lot so they would not further disrupt the students and could regain some composure.

Bo and the pastor waited for a moment in silence, staring at the ground, in hopes of regaining some semblance of sanity. But the minute they looked up at each other, the merriment could not be contained. It started all over again, only this time with the image of those shining faces in the windows spurring them further into unpatrolled hilarity.

After considerable time went by and they were finally able to control themselves, it was Pastor Clover who spoke first.

"I call you Beauregard Lee because that is the name your loving mother gave you. That is your Christian name, and that is the name God heard when you were baptized in yonder creek, just as I was and our entire families were. I call you Beauregard Lee out of respect for your family. Ain't it nice to hear your full name said every now and then, the way your Mama said it?"

Not expecting an answer, he paused for effect. He then stepped a little closer to Bo, placed his hand on his shoulder, and continued his monologue.

"You are fighting a powerful demon, one that eats away at your sleep and thoughts. What happened in 1942 has been over for a very long time. Elijah Waters has moved on and put the past where it belongs.

"You are a good man, and that is why I pray for you every day. You shouldn't carry around the guilt you feel. You should let it go. Everyone else has healed, the pain is gone, and the memories have faded. You should do the same."

At first, Clover did all the talking, and Bo was grateful for it. He didn't know the words that would express his heart, and he would probably just stand around kicking at the grass attempting to formulate a conversation that would never reach a point.

Finally, though, he did speak. "I reckon that's what I came here to say," he conceded, his voice cracking from the weight of his guilt and sadness. His lower lip quivered. As much as Pastor Clover knew, Bo knew the pastor did not know everything about that day in 1942, and he could not bring himself to inform him otherwise.

"You can't make things right with God by giving anonymous gifts to the church," Pastor Clover said.

Bo raised his brow and turned toward the parking lot.

"But you can by talking to Him. He is always willing to listen and forgive. Just like everyone else has already forgiven what happened so long ago," Clover said. He walked Bo through the tattered parking lot. The men shook hands before Bo opened the truck door. He hopped behind the wheel, then turned to look at his friend. Clover flashed a beautiful mouthful of white teeth, framed boldly by his genuine smile, and said, "But if you're so inclined to, say, donate a chain-link fence to the church, we sure would appreciate it. It will keep your cows a lot safer. Lord knows these kids are dangerous—take my word for it." He punctuated the statement by rolling his coal-black pupils upward.

Bo gave a smile, tipped his hat, and replied, "I'll study on it. I suppose it will help protect my cattle, like that septic system."

"How's that, Beauregard?"

"I was afraid one of my cows would fall into the next outhouse hole you dug over by my pasture," Bo stated as he started the truck engine.

"Well, I never thought of it like that," Pastor Clover said with the familiar joy in his voice. "The Lord do work in mysterious ways; mysterious indeed."

# 6

My Darling,

I heard a strange noise in the middle of the night, so I picked up my shotgun and stepped off the back porch toward the barn. I pushed one of the big double doors open with my free hand, and it creaked and moaned with a loud noise, announcing my presence to all the horses resting in the barn. I flipped on the light and scanned the stalls, searching for anything out of place. Each horse stood in its stall, quiet and sleepy-eyed, except for Whisky. He was flat on the ground with his head tilted to one side. Surely, I thought, he must have heard me swing open the barn door.

I called out his name and he did not respond. I dropped my shotgun right there in the dirt a few feet from the door. It's a wonder it did not go off. I rushed over to Whisky, thinking there must be something seriously wrong with him. As I unlatched and swung open the door to his stall, he rose up and greeted me with as perplexed a look that a sleepy horse could give. My darling, I thought he was dead. I held onto his neck and cried with immense relief. I don't know what I would have done if I lost him. Just like I still wonder what I'm doing without you. The only thing keeping me on this wretched earth is an uncompleted task.

I know this to be true because when I returned to the house, I had a spell. I could not breathe. My chest tightened up like a knot in a rope being pulled from both ends. For a moment, I thought: Good, this is my end, and I can go now. I can find comfort.

I fell to the floor clutching my chest. The pain was great and greatly rewarding at the same time. It reminded me that I am alive and now I am going to die. I have felt nothing for so long; it felt good to feel this pain. I stumbled over to the couch and fell on it, thinking to myself, this is where our children will find me. I will look as if I fell asleep and it was a peaceful, comfortable death. I thought how that would have been okay, a fitting place and a fitting way for me to die, instead of stretching out my years and dwindling away as a feeble old man unable to ride and a burden on others. This was a good death.

The phone was only a few inches from my hand. I would let it sit there and not call for help, I thought. I would let this take its course and be done with it. However, I could not do it. I summoned forth a strength in me I did not know I had and denied the wishes of one man for the salvation of another.

# 7

The phone rang in Clint's house just a little past three a.m.

"Wretched contraption! What—? Who—? What time—?"

The sandpaper grit of his voice was amplified by hours of disuse. Clint sat up on the edge of his bed and swung his legs over onto the floor. He paused for a moment and rubbed his knee, trying to calm its painful complaining from being so abruptly awoken and ushered into service without so much as a common alarm-clock warning. The ringing stopped as Clint started to reach for his house slippers to shield his feet from the cold hardwood floors.

Clint had agreed to have the phone installed, at Clay's insistence, after Mary Beth passed away. Practically family, after all, he did live much closer to the ranch than either of Bo's sons. With Bo getting up there in years and manning that property solo, it just made sense to have an extra point of contact. But the phone rarely rang in Clint's house, maybe was used once or twice a week. Though he understood the wisdom of having it, Clint viewed it mostly as an intrusion on the quiet solitude he so cherished. With the night air silent once again, he gave into the pull of sleep and drifted back to his dreams. His slippers still on his feet, he slowly rolled over onto his side with them dangling off the edge of the bed.

"Must've been a dream," he growled and began to kick off his slippers. The ringing pierced the silence again.

"Nope, not a dream."

He sprung to his feet, heading for the front room where the phone sat on top of the lamp table next to his recliner. He made his way to the chair, plopped down in it, turned on the lamp, and picked up the receiver.

"Yes," he said with no hint of his sleepy demeanor.

"Clint." Clay's voice came from the other side of the receiver. "It's Dad. I think something's wrong with him. He might be having a heart attack. I called an ambulance. I don't have much more information than that; however, I am on my way over there. Can you meet me there?" he asked, his matter-of-fact tone coated with concern.

"Yeah, I can be there in just a few minutes. I will call you when I get there."

"You'll have to speak to my wife when you call; I'll be on my way."

Clint hung up the phone, hastily put on his clothes, and staggered off the front porch in his house slippers, taking only enough time to grab his cowboy hat. It took him just five minutes to get to the ranch house, where he didn't even bother knocking before he entered. Bo was sitting on the couch in his front parlor. A lamp and its small table had been knocked over, splayed across the floor. Bo was still in his bed clothes and confused, but recognized Clint as he came through the front door.

"What are you doing here so early?" Bo asked in a voice that was shaky and broken.

It was immediately obvious to Clint that Bo was disoriented and had no idea what was going on.

"Could you do me a favor, Clint? Pick up that lamp and put it back on the table. I've been trying to get up out of this couch and do it myself, but my legs don't seem to work."

"Sure, I'll do that for you." Clint bent at the knees to right the table, watching the old man carefully, trying to figure what to do next.

———•———

Bo slowly shook away the cobwebs from his mind, slowly

recalling the events of the last few hours. He remembered calling Clay first and then his younger son Jeb. However, he was still a bit confused as to why Clint was bent down in his living room picking up an overturned end table.

"You're wearing house slippers," Bo remarked, the sight of which did not help his confused state. "The livestock is going to think you have lost your marbles." He chuckled weakly.

"It's fitting attire," Clint commented in a wry tone, "for this time of day . . . I mean, night."

Bo pieced the puzzle together with every bit of information he received. He reached over to pick up the phone base, pulling on the trailing cord and receiver that lay on the floor at his feet. Then he was reminded of the pain, intense and alarming, and immediately the picture snapped into place. He started to rise.

"Whoa, whoa, now you just sit still, lean back, and put your feet up on the coffee table," Clint ordered, taking the phone from Bo's hands.

Bo did as he was told, offering no resistance to Clint's directions. The pain that lingered in his left arm and chest made him grimace, but he did not cry out. He shook his head and replied, "That smarts right much."

Clint placed the phone back on the lamp stand, clicking the receiver in place. The instant he did that, the phone started to ring. When Bo leaned to his right and started to reach for it, Clint gave him another stern look.

"I'll do that."

"I can get it. My right arm is fine," Bo said loudly, but with little punch behind the words.

"You are the orneriest thing. Sit still and let me tend to you."

"Fine," the old man replied as Clint picked up the phone just short of the third ring.

———◦———

"Dad," Jeb's voice came quickly.

"No sir, this is Clint."

"Oh, Clint, I couldn't get through. Is Daddy okay?"

"Yeah, looks like he's going to be fine."

"Are you sure? Is the ambulance there yet?" Jeb asked.

"No, not yet, and I'm sure he ain't going to like that," Clint said.

"Can he talk? Let me talk to him," Jeb said.

"I ain't going to like what?" Bo quickly asked.

"An ambulance ride," Clint said as he moved around the coffee table to hand the receiver to his boss. "Here. It's your son Jeb."

Bo reached out his right arm and took the receiver from Clint. "I'm not getting in an ambulance. People die in those things."

"Yes you are, Daddy," Jeb replied strongly.

"I'll have Clint drive me to the hospital in the morning. I'll be fine."

"Absolutely not; give the phone back to Clint, Daddy," Jeb ordered.

Clint was awkwardly attempting to prop up Bo's legs with a pillow on the coffee table. Dispensing with the kid gloves, he finally swooped his forearm under both legs and guided the pillow underneath them with the other.

"Here, he wants to talk to you. I ain't going in no ambulance. What are you doing? Stop that, my legs ain't broke." Bo held out the receiver.

Jeb overheard the conversation and commented, "It sounds like he's not that bad off."

"No sir, he's fighting me every step of the way, so I'm sure he'll be okay." Clint turned in Bo's direction and gave him a look.

"Okay, I will meet you at the hospital later. Clay should get there before the ambulance, but if he doesn't, would you ride with him in the ambulance?" Jeb asked.

"Yes sir, I'll do that for you."

"Thank you, Clint. I don't know what we would do without you. Daddy can be an enormous pain sometimes."

"Sometimes?" Clint replied with exaggerated bewilderment.

Jeb thanked him again and hung up the phone. Clint paused for a few seconds and then began to speak into the phone, pretending to still be talking to Jeb.

"Okay. Yes sir. He ain't going to like that at all. Yes, we have one out in the barn. We use it on the horses. The hose is a might big, but I suppose it will fit. It will take some pushing. Yes, I understand."

Bo's face twisted into a giant question mark as Clint hung up the phone, pushed back his cowboy hat, and started to scratch the top of his head.

"I know that look, Clint. What are you up to?" Bo asked with liveliness in his voice.

"Jeb just got off the phone with the doctors over at Hermann Hospital. He knew you would start bucking like a bronco when it came to an ambulance ride."

Bo's eyes pinched down to a fine slit, his pupils, barely visible. He was hunkering down like a badger, intent on having his way.

"He said you could come in on your own tomorrow morning."

"Good," Bo blurted out, victoriously crossing his arms.

"But . . ." Clint said and then turned away as if that was the end of the conversation. He strolled over to the window, nonchalantly pulled the curtains aside with two fingers, and bent his head forward.

"But?" Bo said.

Clint ignored him and continued staring through the small opening in the drapes.

"*But*. You said *but*. But what? And what's all that stuff about the horses and a hose?"

Clint had his full attention now. "Oh, I said *butt*."

"Yes, I heard you say but. That's what I'm asking you: but what?"

"No, not that kind of *but*. We're talking about your b-u-t-t, *butt*."

Bo's eyes were as large as the headlights on his pickup truck.

"What are you talking about, Clint?" Bo insisted.

"The doctors said they would give you an exam at the hospital and a few pills to swallow that would make you better. And that they wanted to keep you overnight, in case you had another spell. Or . . ." Clint trailed off from the conversation.

"Or what?"

"Or we could use an old home remedy that would hold you over until tomorrow morning. I got everything we need out in the barn, except for liquid soap. You got any in the kitchen?" Clint asked and started to walk into the kitchen.

"What are you talking about?" Clint could sense the anger in Bo's voice building.

"Oh, and can you walk? Because we have to—oh, here it is," Clint hollered from the kitchen as he noisily rummaged around in the cabinet underneath Bo's sink. He then returned to the parlor with a plastic bottle of lemon-scented Joy. "We can't do this in the house. It's going to make a big mess."

"All right now, that's enough. I've had enough. You tell me right now what you're talking about!" Bo ordered sternly, glaring at Clint, who was standing in front of him with a bottle of liquid soap.

"The enema," Clint explained, holding out his left hand, inviting Bo to stand.

Bo choked on disbelief and confusion.

"Of course, we will have to do this over by the clothesline away from the barn. I can hang the enema bag on the wire and your clothes on it afterward. We'll be around the corner so as the horses won't see. No need in embarrassing yourself in front of the livestock."

Bo's face started to soften, and his eyes relaxed as he realized what Clint was doing.

"All right," he said softly.

"Now come on, the sooner we get this over with, the better. I'd like to go home to that warmth of my bed."

"I'll ride in the ambulance," Bo said in a low and somber voice.

"What's that you say?" Clint said jokingly, shaking the bottle of soap. "It's lemony fresh. You'll smell like clean dishes, and you'll fart bubbles."

Bo chuckled mildly and shook his head. "I'm starting to look forward to an ambulance ride. At least I stand a chance of surviving, and it'll get me away from you."

"I'll bet," Clint replied as he laughed and turned to answer the knocking at the front door.

Clay arrived a few short minutes after the ambulance. By the time he'd entered the house, Bo had already been loaded onto the gurney and was being rolled out of the house. Clint gathered up a few items of clothing, along with Bo's shaving gear and emerged from Bo's bedroom to find Clay astonished to see his father willingly accepting an ambulance ride. The medics informed Clay that it would be fine for him to follow in his truck—his father was safe. The heart attack was apparently a mild one.

Clay asked Clint if he would lock everything up at the ranch before returning home. Clint said he would. Clay thanked him once again and asked, "Oh by the way, how on earth did you get the old bull to lie down and get in that ambulance without a fight?"

"It's an old horse trick I learned a long time ago. I'll tell you about it one day, after I've caught up on my sleep," Clint promised.

# 8

Within a few weeks Bo grew tired of being looked after like a child. The walls closed in on him as if he were imprisoned. Between Clint, his daughters-in-law, and his sons, he was about to go crazy. Every morning when Bo got up, one of the family was lingering in the kitchen or some other part of the house, offering help with this or with that. The icebox had so much food in it he had to give some away to Clint and Matt just to be able to close the door. And someone was always in the house—a reality that he was not used to and did not prefer. His laundry was done, his dishes were cleaned, his floors were swept, and the rainbow of pills he was forced to take every day were given to him along with a glass of water four times a day, all like clockwork.

He had not realized the enjoyment he'd felt in his solitude until it was so abruptly taken from him. He felt invaded; though he enjoyed his loved one's company and attention, it was just far too much and for the wrong reason. They hovered like worker bees, buzzing with annoying questions like: *How do you feel? Are you in pain? Can I get you anything special from the store? Is the house too hot or cold for you?* Queries and concerned faces were everywhere. The phone rang like a bell on a lead cow's neck every time it took a step. Bo became convinced that the cure and the care were far worse than the illness itself.

To make matters worse, he was neglecting his Whisky, who would wander through the center of the barn up to the back porch in search of Bo. Clint would fetch him back after Bo gave him a slice of apple and an apology for his absence along with a rub on his neck. Clint would ride the horse short distances, like to the end of the driveway to retrieve the mail, but the discomfort from the old knee injuries would not allow longer jaunts.

On the third week of his convalescence, Bo rose from his bed to find his house empty of eager caregivers. He slowly crept through the rooms, certain one of them would emerge from behind the door or hallway holding a glass of water in one hand and a fistful of pills in the other. Bo shuffled in his slippers along the hardwood floors to the kitchen. On the small table against the wall, he found a note from Kate, Clay's wife. She'd started him a pot of coffee and set aside the pills he was to take, along with instructions for the day. The note said she would return around noon to check on him and make lunch. *A perfect opportunity for escape,* he thought. He quickly gobbled down the three pills left in a dish next to his empty coffee cup. He walked to the sink and filled the cup with tap water to help swallow the pills. As he drank the water with his left hand, he poured out the coffee pot with his right into the sink. Kate's coffee was horrible, worse than his own, and he'd always make up a polite excuse why he did not want any each time she offered him a cup. He raced back to his bedroom and quickly changed into his faded Levi jeans and canvas, button-down, long-sleeved shirt, placed socks on his feet, and made a hasty dash for the back porch to retrieve his well-worn Tony Lamas.

"Oh no!" he said aloud, realizing his riding boots were not where they should be. "She's hidden my riding boots."

Kate was smart, he knew. She probably figured if she was not watching her father-in-law like a hawk, he would venture out to the barn and eventually into the saddle. She'd hidden those boots somewhere, hoping to slow him down until she returned. He was determined to foil her plan.

———•———

Clint chuckled and shook his head as he observed Bo through

open blinds along the windows at the back of the house. The old man darted back and forth with surprising speed and agility. He knew the old man was searching for his boots.

Finally Bo emerged from the house again, this time holding a pair of boots that were not his riding boots, but a pair he usually wore around the house and yard. *Determined*, Clint thought.

Clint held a pair of boots in his hands as well—the treasured riding boots. He had cleaned and brushed them down. All the dirt that normally clung to the edges between the sole and the stitching work was gone, and a fresh polish had been applied. The polish absorbed into the roughness of the well-worn leather, leaving behind an attractive luster.

"Your boots," Clint said as he approached the back porch. He grinned at Bo. "She told me to hide them from you, but I figured it's better to just give them to you so you don't scuff up another pair."

Bo took them from Clint and sat down, placing his good boots on the porch chair next to him. He pressed his feet into the old ones. They slid on just as easily and comfortable as his socks. Bo stood slowly and looked down from the porch at his friend. Before he could say thank you, Clint said, "You better get. You know how Kate is, and she could be back any minute."

"You're right," Bo said agreeably. He sprang to his feet and made some lively steps across the yard toward the barn. When he reached Whisky's stall, it was empty.

"He's saddled up around back, and he's a lot more excited about going for a ride than you are," Clint said as he entered the barn. "And if they ask, I'm going to tell them you threatened to fire me."

They shared a knowing glance that was as rich as their friendship. No further explanation was needed. Bo tipped his hat and disappeared through the barn doors.

# 9

Bo woke at his usual time and made his way into the kitchen to start the morning coffee. The light was already on in the barn, and he could see Clint standing in front of the chalkboard, black cowboy hat in his hands. No doubt he was wondering why Whisky was not to be saddled for his regular morning ride. Bo had decided to spend the day ruminating over what to do about Elijah Waters. The time he'd spent with Pastor Clover had left him with many questions that he struggled to answer.

The coffeemaker completed filling the first morning pot. Bo poured a steaming cup and brought it with him into the living room. Lifting the cup to his lips, he gently blew over the edge of the mug in an attempt to cool it. He took a sip, then hacked and grimaced in protest of his own coffee-making abilities—or inabilities.

"It still tastes like warm cow piss. If I don't figure this out, I may never drink a cup of joe again. Honey, I wish I knew what you did to your coffee to make it taste so incredible," he mumbled as he placed the cup on the corner of the desk.

His thoughts drifted back to the many mornings he'd hurried out of the house and into the barn to start the day's work. Mary Beth was always up before him, preparing his coffee along with a small sack lunch that he would carry in his saddlebag or on the front seat of his truck. They were little things that he'd taken for granted and, of course, were now remarkably missed.

Bo also wished he had indulged himself more in Mary Beth's smile and pleasing company. It was their conversations that he missed the most, at dinnertime usually. He looked forward to his daily greeting upon entering their impeccable home at the end of the day—impeccable because of Mary Beth—and the warm smells coming from the kitchen. Yes, it had been their favorite time together when the workday came to an end. Bo would remove his boots on the back porch, and Mary Beth would offer him a cool glass of iced tea or a hot cup of coffee, depending on the season. She was always sensitive to the needs of her hard-working, rancher husband.

"I wish I could see you again, Mary Beth, and kiss your warm cheek. And in that stolen moment, I would ask you: *what is your secret for making coffee taste so wonderful?"*

Leaning over his coffee, he reached for a manila folder and opened it—gently, as it contained precious information. He stared intently at the data he'd requested from his son, Clay, who'd been glad to help with the research. Laid before him was information on Elijah Waters: his address, phone number, and history. All the intelligence that Bo needed to contact Elijah was there, neatly organized, waiting to be put to use—a decision that was Bo's alone. Paper-clipped to the sheets of Elijah's history was a handwritten note on yellow legal-pad paper: "Dad, if there is anything else I can do for you, please let me know. If this is something you would like the firm to handle for you, we can make it happen. Clay."

Of course, Clay would have an inkling of what his father was up to, surely having read the history himself, as any prudent lawyer, or son, would do. But Bo had never shared with him the more tragic side of his involvement with Elijah Waters. Bo removed one of the sheets of paper and studied it, leaning back into the soft leather of his chair. He reached up and pulled the lamp closer to him. The slumbering sun had not yet produced enough light to fill the room, but he did not want false light. So he studied the text with some strain on his eyes, which was ironically quite appropriate. As he read, the words pulled like chains, dragging across a floor of cold and dirty concrete, creating a horrific symphony of despair and agony. And he was doing the draggin', those chains tightly affixed to his soul.

Lies. Preserved on paper, stored in a filing cabinet, and archived permanently for historical reference. This was an injustice that needed reversal, and Bo knew he was the only person who could right the wrong. Even though Elijah Waters had been found not guilty of the theft, for four decades, Bo had harbored within himself the arrogant belief that he was the victim of this innocent man.

Bo rose from his chair and headed out the door toward the barn. Time for a change.

# 10

Clint stepped a little closer to the fence line, squinting. It was still dark out there in the pasture, which made it difficult to count the head of cattle. It would be another twenty minutes or so before he put out the feed and four bales of hay, but the cows had arrived early, as always. One was missing. Clint again counted, lost track, stepped closer to the fence, and resumed the count. The cows at the hay drop, farther back from the trough, were harder to see not just because of the lack of light, but also because they weren't standing shoulder to shoulder like the cattle waiting at the feed trough.

*It's just too dark*, he thought as he turned to walk back to the barn. He saw Bo leaning over the hitching post just outside the main door. Holding a cup of coffee in both hands, he'd been observing Clint trying to count heads. Clint pushed his cowboy hat halfway back on his head and scratched his scalp. He mumbled, "Got to wait." He walked closer to Bo. "I think we're missing a cow."

"You sure?" Bo asked.

"Nope, but I will be after I've had a cup of coffee. Maybe it will wake me up, and by that time, it will be lighter."

Bo leaned easily over the hitching post, peering for a few moments into the pasture dark. After another sip of the coffee, he poured the remainder onto the ground, holding the cup upside down until the last drop fell. He then followed Clint to a small room just inside the main barn door. It was Clint's office, furnished sparingly with the usual office lineup, including a tall filing cabinet. All records on the animals, along with documentation on equipment and ranch hands, were kept there in Clint's usual organized fashion. On a small table just inside the door was a coffee pot from which Clint poured a cup. A hot, white cloud of steam rose up from the mug and floated around Clint's face as he took a sip. He offered some to Bo, who declined. The two of them made small talk as they patiently waited for the sun to rise and provide them enough light to effectively count the cattle.

Bo asked Clint, "Have you seen a young colored boy running around with a fishing pole?"

"Yep, I see him most every Saturday running across the backside of the pasture. Always toting a small box and a fishing pole. He's easy to see as he runs through the tall grass with the bobber at the end of his fishing pole bouncing up and down. He seems harmless enough," Clint concluded as he focused his eyes on the ever-brightening dawn, concentrating on the pasture and his final sip of coffee.

A long pause, then Bo responded, "Yeah, I saw him for the first time the other day, like you say, bouncing up and down across the pasture on his way to the creek. He stopped just before he crossed the creek and waved both arms at me in an attempt to get my attention. I just sort of tipped my hat and let him go. What harm can one young black boy do?"

Clint took another sip of coffee and, without turning to look at Bo, remarked, "There was a day when you would have run off the black folk congregating for a baptism in the creek. I think you're slowing down just like that old rooster."

"Yep, I reckon those days are long past. It takes me awhile to gather up enough steam to do much of anything these days."

As if on cue, a lone rooster announced the rising of the sun.

"It's a good thing we don't rely on that bird to get us up in the morning. I swear he crows later every day."

"Yep, he's getting old and slow. Won't be long before a fox gets him. He's gotten to where it's hard for him to get up in the trees at night to roost, and he is still too cantankerous to lock up in the henhouse. You sure you don't want a cup of my coffee?"

"Got my own inside, thanks."

"Suit yourself," Clint replied. They stood quietly in the growing dawn, taking in the serenity of the quiet, early summer's morning. Within ten minutes, there was ample light for them to count that cattle, which they each quietly did. Bo was the first to speak.

"Better saddle up Whisky. It looks like I'll be taking a ride after all."

Clint agreed—one short of thirteen.

———•———

Bo returned to the house to put on his Lamas, their leather so soft and supple that they flopped over and touched the floor when not stuck on Bo's legs. The heels, having been re-soled often over the years, fit the stirrups perfectly, giving him a strong grip. They were also slanted in a little, giving spurs a better angle at a horse's belly to tickle or abruptly jab the soft hide, depending on the amount of convincing necessary to motivate the horse. However, Bo never wore spurs on any of his horses these days. Spurs were for the young cowboys, muscled and brave enough to mount an arrogant stud and convince him to obey. Those days had long since passed for Bo.

He poured himself another cup of coffee and took it back to the barn with him. He walked through the barn this time, to the far end, and there he surveyed the herd. He sipped from his mug. The look of displeasure quickly followed as he choked down another mouthful of the liquid.

"Man, that's tough to take!" he remarked, and resigned, he once again flung the coffee onto the ground just outside the barn.

"It's Sally," Clint said as he reached over to finish cinching up Whisky's saddle.

"What's that?"

"I said it's Sally II that's missing. I figure she had her calf last night some time and is laid down somewhere with it. I noticed yesterday after I fed them all that she sort of separated from the herd."

"Well, that makes sense. I'll go find her and bring back the calf. She'll follow us in."

"You want a cup of coffee?" Clint said, poking fun at his friend.

"What?" Bo was oblivious. He stared in the direction of the far corner of the main pasture. About half a mile away, a truck had turned onto the dirt road that led to the house. It was Matt, late as usual. The lights of the truck bounced up and down as if he were driving over a freshly plowed cornfield.

"That boy is going to kill himself or someone else if he doesn't slow down."

"It's not him I'm worried about—it's the cows. You want me to fire him?" Clint asked with a hint of hope in his tone.

"No, just tell him to slow down."

"It would be easier to fire him. Coffee?"

"No."

"No to the coffee? Or firing the boy?"

"No to both, and I'm sure your coffee is just as bad as mine."

"Suit yourself," Clint replied.

With practiced ease, Bo swung himself atop Whisky and headed into the pasture.

"Where you going in such a hurry?" Bo asked his horse, who had picked up his pace to a canter. He often had discussions with his equine partner. "Whoa now, just you stop right there," he ordered, pulling back on the reins. "I want to search the front pasture first, along the tree line, before we head over to the other side of the creek."

Whisky cranked his ears around as if to better hear what Bo had just said. At least he appeared to be listening. "Now giddyup." Bo let out the reins and gave Whisky a light leg command to the left. The horse snorted and jerked his head.

Then Clint sounded off from behind him.

"He's got a notion in his head! He was like that the entire time I was saddling him up! You might want to let him go his own way!"

Bo turned in the saddle to better address Clint over his left shoulder.

"You reckon?" Bo let the reins out again, and Whisky turned toward the bridge and resumed the canter.

"Yep, I reckon," Clint said as he indulged himself in a few final moments of quiet solitude before Matt stumbled into the barn with his excuse for being late.

# 11

Whisky slowed at the end of the trail that led them to the grove where wildflowers bloomed. Their brilliance of color in numbers too large to count had always been a welcome sight for Bo and his family. This part of the property used to be one of his grandchildren's favorite places, before they'd gotten so busy with school and more urban activities. They would always stop at that spot during weekend horseback rides and sit on one of the benches placed at the edge of the creek bank, or at the top of the hill where the blanket of flowers started. The graveyard sat atop that hill, a small plot of scattered gravestones marking the resting places of his family as far back as his grandfather Jebediah and as recent as his sweet Mary Beth.

Cattle had grazed in it for several years until Mary Beth insisted that he erect a fence around the plot to keep them out. He had not put much effort into it: just several cedar fence posts placed in the ground around the grave sites with two strands of barbed wire at the top. He'd included a small rickety gate just large enough for one person coming or going.

But after his wife was buried there, Bo had asked his sons to find a company to install an ornate, black, wrought iron fence with an elaborate double gate. The gate swung wide like an inviting hug. Above the gate was an archway that spread like a rainbow as it flowed from one side to the other.

One afternoon, while writing in his journal and sitting alone on the stone bench inside the new fence, he had looked up and noticed, for the first time, the flower shapes molded into the black metal. His gaze held fast the artistry he had not noticed before. *Oh God, how could I have missed such a beautiful sight? I have been a fool for far too long, and a blind one at that. I should have paid closer attention to what was going on, instead of just ordering something to be done.*

Bo's eyes had filled with tears that overflowed onto his sun-roughened cheeks. It was then he realized how impersonal he had been toward an intensely personal place. His loving sons had been listening to the stories Mary Beth had shared—about how she and their father had met and would spend hours together on the creek bank surrounded by flowers.

After discovering the intricate designs in the archway, he had returned the next day with several bags of wildflower seeds and tools in the back of his truck and started turning up the rich soil around the perimeter of the graveyard. The soil was so rich and generous with compost that the seeds sprouted from the ground in only a few days. Over the past three years, they'd spread like wildfire in every direction with no further tending. They crept through the iron fence and across the grave sites, coloring the place in blues, pinks, and yellows during the summer. In the winter, the colors would change to flowers of brilliant orange and shades of red. The flowers were now so thick that the roots bound together and strangled out the weeds to leave behind a knee-high spectacle of floral joy.

As Bo meandered through his memories, Whisky grazed on his own, occasionally eyeing his emotional friend. Finally, the horse walked over to Bo, placing his muzzle near to his face. Bo lifted his arm and rubbed Whisky's jawline. "I'm okay, old friend," he replied as Whisky stood silent, still, and strong.

Inexplicably, Bo's line of sight was drawn downfield. Far off in the right-hand corner of the pasture, close to the creek, Bo could see that the flowers were uprooted, along with the turf and parts of the barbed wire fence.

It was there that Bo found Sally II tangled in the fence.

# 12

"This is such an enormous waste of time," Matt complained as he picked up a shovel from the back of the truck and started walking over to the dead cow and her calf.

The buzzards had fled when Matt and Clint approached in the pickup truck. Some circled and others, burdened with the weight of the flesh they had gorged upon, perched in the tops of the trees, waiting for their chance to resume the feast.

Bo had sent the men out to free Sally II from the barbed wire fence and bury her next to the spot where he'd put her down.

"We should just roll what's left of the cow into the creek, or better yet, let the buzzards finish her off. Hell, even buzzards got to eat."

"You just start digging a hole and be thankful that the soil is soft and sandy down here by the creek," Clint replied, throwing a look of disgust in Matt's direction.

"Why are you looking at me like that for? It's just a dead cow. It ain't like it's his best friend or something like that."

"Look up there on the hill, boy." Clint turned toward the graveyard and pointed. "His whole family is buried up there, including his wife Mary Beth. Would you want this next to your loved ones?"

"They're dead. It don't really matter much. Once you're dead, you're dead."

"You've got a lot more to learn about the living before you can make a statement like that. When you look down, all you see is a dead cow. But when the boss saw this, I'm sure it tore him up inside. He won't forget what he saw here because this is more than just a cow to him. It's a part of him and it's a part of his family—even though, as you say, it's just a cow. Now dig, and dig deep enough so it don't get dug up by the critters."

Within forty-five minutes they had the hole deep and wide enough for Sally II, with her calf still in womb. Clint returned from the truck with a set of posthole diggers and a pair of wire cutters. He reset the posts and repaired the wire. He then turned to Matt, who'd started to walk off toward the truck with both the shovels, and hollered, "You need to smooth this off so there is no hump in the dirt. It needs to look as if this never happened."

"Geez, if we're going to go through all that trouble, why don't I just go up to the graveyard and fetch a stone for it?" Matt dropped one of the shovels, stomped back down toward the creek with the other shovel, and started flinging dirt in all directions in order to smooth off the top of the mound. Clint resisted the urge to say anything for a few moments as he observed Matt throwing his little tantrum. Once Clint had calmed himself down and gathered his thoughts, he picked up the other shovel and assisted Matt.

"Do you know what compassion means, boy?"

"Yeah, but I don't see how compassion can apply to a dead cow."

"The dead cow is a metaphor of how the boss's life is going right now. He's lost without his wife, and he only gets to see his family when they feel like coming down here to the ranch. Besides that, something else has been burning in him awful hard. The fire in his belly is so bad he can't find much comfort in anything he does. Seeing this cow struggle and suffer like it did probably felt like a red-hot poker thrust in him.

"If you were here on time, you would have seen what I saw in his eyes when he set off on Whisky to find Sally II and her new calf. He was a young cowboy again, sitting tall and proud in the saddle, gone off to fetch back a shiny new calf. It was the first time I've seen him that happy in a long, long time. I poured myself a cup of coffee and made my way over to the edge of the bridge in order to see firsthand the look on his face when he crossed the bridge with a pretty new calf slung across the front of his saddle. And that's when I heard it." Clint became quiet as he bent down and picked up the remainder of the tools and started toward the truck.

"Heard what?" Matt asked as he followed close behind Clint. Clint, however, did not speak until he was sitting in the truck and Matt had closed the door on his side.

"The sound of his pistol. It meant only one thing, and I knew it right away. That's why I returned to my office and waited."

For the first time, Matt was quiet, as if he were taking it all in and it was starting to make sense to him.

"I didn't hear a pistol."

"That's because you weren't listening, just like you're not listening now."

# 13

When they arrived back at the ranch house, Clint backed the truck up to the opened end of the barn, between the main house and the barn door. Bo was sitting on the back porch, his reading glasses perched on his nose, writing in his journal. He looked in Clint's direction, and the two of them made eye contact. Clint slightly nodded his head as Bo returned the glance, lifting his coffee cup and taking a sip. There was no need for words; each understood the other as old friends did. Bo then poured out his coffee in the flowerbed, leaned back in the chair, and continued to write.

Clint entered the barn to his office. He grabbed the simmering coffee pot in one hand, cup in the other, and walked to the house and onto the porch.

"Here," Clint said as he picked up Bo's coffee cup and filled it from his pot. "I watched you pour out three cups of coffee this morning. I think it's time you tried mine. You might find a familiar taste in it."

Clint then poured another cup for himself and set the pot down on a small table. Bo lifted the cup to his mouth and took a sip. His brow did not wrinkle nor did he wince in disgust. Instead he looked up at Clint with surprise and a smile.

"That tastes exactly like Mary Beth's coffee! I didn't know you knew her recipe."

"That's because you never asked," Clint said as he gave a small grin in Bo's direction, then walked back to the barn with just his coffee cup in hand.

"Aren't you going to tell me how to get my coffee to taste like this?"

"Nope!" Clint never broke stride, but hollered loud enough for Bo to hear, "If I do that, I'll never be able to get you out of that house. You know where my coffee pot is, so help yourself."

Bo leaned back in his chair and held the cup close to his chin, inhaling an aroma that could change his whole mood. He picked up his pen and began to write.

My Dearest Love Mary Beth,

I came across a sight that I have witnessed many times since I was a young boy. However, the effect on me has changed. I found one of the heifers tangled up in barbed wire on the backside of Clear Creek early this morning. She was just a few hundred feet from the graveyard, by the open meadow where we used to meet in the early evenings to watch the sun as it sank down over the tall pines . . . the place where I gathered up the gumption to tell you I loved you for the first time. I remember the smile you returned reassured me that you loved me too, even though you didn't say it back.

In that spot, where the buttercups and bluebonnets spread out like a pink and blue carpet hundreds of yards wide all the way down to the creek bank's edge, a horrible sight awaited me, Mary Beth. Our six-year-old whiteface cow, Sally II, struggled in her final moments of life. Her back legs were tangled in the fence, and a dead breached calf was hanging from her backside. Judging from the scuffed up sod and uprooted fence posts, she must have struggled for hours. Her entangled legs were cut to the bone, and the blood was dry and thick with dust and flies. The buzzards were already working on the dead calf and attempting to tear at the heifer's hide. I knew right off that there was no saving her.

I rode up to her on Whisky. He didn't like those buzzards. I could tell because he snorted and charged at them. There were about thirty of them hovering around the heifer and her calf. Their heads bobbed up and down, wings spread, as they pulled and jerked at the flesh of the suffering cow. They looked like a black cloud of death.

This gruesome sight I have seen before with younger eyes, but its effect on me now . . . and it took all my strength to haul back on Whisky's reins as he stomped and snorted.

As buzzards scattered and fled, one of them turned into the wind that was blowing up from behind me. His belly was so swollen and fat he had to flap his wings furiously in order to get into the air. He flew so close to my head that his wings almost touched me. I felt the swell of the air and heard his wings as they beat against his chest. I am convinced that if death had a sound, that is what it would sound like.

The dried blood reminded me of the day the sheriff's deputies beat and tormented Elijah Waters. I did not feel his pain then because of my arrogance and hatred. But now my calloused emotions have softened with age. I feel what I should have felt then, pain like shards of broken glass scraping against my memories, awakening the compassion I should have had all along.

I dismounted and approached Sally II, struggling with what I knew must be done. It is funny how sensitive my emotions have become; this simple act of mercy tore at my heart. It was as if I could feel her pain and anguish, and, at the same time, her welcoming the mercy of death. It wasn't that way when I was younger and walked in the boots of my youth. Why is God so cruel that he would allow such a thing, especially in this place that has been a haven for me since your passing? Now, here where our lives first began under the setting sun and the blooming flowers, the rippling waters of the creek will never be able to drown out the sound of the buzzard's wings as they fled Whisky's hooves. It is desecrated with an agonizing death and the sound of my pistol as it cracked through the morning air.

Perhaps it is my fault, Mary Beth. I knew Sally II was close to her time. Maybe I should have kept her home so I could keep my eyes on her better. I told myself it would be okay, because this was not her first calf. All I know now is this hurts, and death has another sound I won't soon forget.

# 14

The barn had always been a refuge for Clint. His mornings and late afternoons were spent doing the things he loved, easily passing away the hours into years working for the Kelso family. His world was in perfect harmony, and his life ambitions met. He had enough of everything he needed. He prided himself on being content with his life. He was at that perfect balance between his past, present, and future, sitting at a point that suited his nature. His salary paid by the estate was more than enough to pay his bills. Frugal in nature, his only bills were household expenses and maintenance on his twenty-year-old Chevy short-bed truck. He'd bought it with the money he received after his injuries working for the traveling rodeo. The rest of the settlement money was in the bank.

In stark contrast to the peace of his current perch, there was the Clint of just about a decade ago. He remembered with disdain those mornings, clouded by the fog of liquor and the effort involved in surviving another day surrounded by the inherited property and home of his only brother.

A few weeks after his brother had died, Clint's mother warned him not to let the bottle take him too. "I don't know why the men in our family fall to the wickedness of liquor; first your father and now your brother. I thought he would learn after watching your father suffer from his failing liver, but it is our doom," she'd said to Clint as they sat on the porch of his dead brother's house.

Clint reassured her that he was not going to fall to the same ruin as his brother and father before him. However, it was a promise he'd already known he would break. After his mother left that afternoon, he closed the door and turned on the TV. He then retrieved a bottle of whisky from a well-stocked cabinet and submerged himself in it, pulling the cork in behind him. His life faded further each day into self-inflicted despair. His plans for the future had been simple: stay locked up in his personal prison and medicate his crippled knee with pity and whisky.

His daily tasks were easy enough. He came to each morning in a haze, fed the two horses that used to be his brother's, then returned to the house to drink the remainder of the day away. At the end of the week, he would drive into town and purchase groceries along with a healthy supply of liquor to get through the next week. On Saturdays, he occupied the same barstool in the same bar until they closed at three in the morning. He repeated this treacherous routine for eight months, until the turning point.

One Saturday night in April, Clint had driven home a little drunker than usual. Stepping out of his truck, he lost his balance and fell to the ground, where he passed out and remained the entire night.

The horses in the small stable behind the house woke him with their incessant whinnying and snorting in an effort to motivate him to bring their breakfast. The mare was a fine Thoroughbred and her foal was about two years old. Both horses were all that remained of his brother's stock legacy. Also a working cowboy, his brother would hire out to ranches during roundups all over the state of Texas, Louisiana, Oklahoma, and New Mexico. He, too, loved his job, traveling and assisting with roundups and sometimes working for traveling rodeos like Clint. The two horses that remained were now Clint's to do with whatever he wished; however, the injuries to his knee kept him from riding.

From the cool ground that morning, Clint had lifted his head, the sounds from the horses flushing the fog from his mind. As if climbing from a hole, he crawled his way to the edge of the truck, placing one hand on top of the tire and the other on top of the hood. He then pulled himself up on his good leg and struggled to bend the other and bring it underneath him to sturdy himself and stand upright. As he did this, the fog returned and his face flushed. He lost his balance, falling over backward onto the ground. He let go of everything at that moment—his strength, his desire, his resolve—and started to cry.

*Oh God, what have I become?* Tears streaming down his face, he managed to roll onto one side. He pulled his knees to his chest, rolled onto his knees, and crawled to the edge of the porch, dragging his bad leg. The cold had set into his bones. Everything ached, but mostly his knee, as he placed one hand over the other and pulled himself up the handrail and onto the front porch. He swung his body around when he got to the top step and sat upright for a moment. Then he leaned forward, placed his hands over his face, and wept like a child. He recognized his despair.

Thoughts flashed through his mind—thoughts that he should fight to keep away, but he did not. He allowed his mind to search for an end to his self-inflicted suffering. He did not use his rational thought, which was far too difficult. He did not consider asking for help: *I can solve my own problems.* He did not think of his mother, nor did he think of his friends, because he had none. All his friends had moved on with the rodeo when it moved to the next town. He only thought of ending the agony he felt. That is when he thought of the single-barrel shotgun behind the bathroom door.

When his tears ran dry on his face, he stumbled into the house. Upon entering the kitchen, he passed up the cereal bowl for a breakfast of booze. The bottle felt comfortable in his shaking hand. He carried it with him into the bathroom, sat on the toilet, pulled out the cork, and lifted the bottle to his lips. He took a long pull. Bubbles danced inside the bottle when he hoisted it up. He lowered the bottle, dangled it between his knees. Head down, he stretched out his right leg and swung the bathroom door shut. It slammed against the frame and latched.

Behind it was the single-barrel shotgun that had belonged to his brother.

"That's what I need right there," he said aloud, the sound of his voice strange, thick and cold. "It'll be better if I do it this way instead of dying by the bottle, slowly dwindling away, listening to my mother's voice in my head. Hell, I'm dead anyway."

He leaned forward to grasp the shotgun. Before his fingers touched it, the horses out back began a raucous protest, whinnying together as loudly as he'd ever heard them. Clint bargained with himself. He would give this dying a deadline. First he would sell the horses, and then he would reconsider his options.

He took a second pull from the bottle and sat back on the toilet. He reached down to the floor, retrieved the cork, and pushed it back into the bottle. The sound of the cork twisting its way into the neck of the bottle was like a comforting song. So familiar to him, the sound was a prelude to that first long drink that calmed his nerves and steadied his hand and, a few drinks later, filled him with soothing comfort.

"All right, I'm coming!" he yelled out the bathroom window so the horses would calm down.

The next day Clint placed an ad in the local newspaper advertising the mare and the two-year-old for sale. He did not have a telephone at the house, so the ad came with directions to his ten-acre farm, which was located not more than a few miles from the Kelso Ranch.

# 15

Mary Beth Kelso sat in the kitchen with her husband, both of them quietly thumbing through the newspapers. An ad caught her eye.

*Two chestnut cutters for sale, one saddle-broke mare and her two-year-old, needs training and a good home. Free. Bring your own trailer.*

Mary Beth's eyes widened with excitement, and she quickly removed the page from the paper.

"Now what are you doing there?" Bo asked his wife, curious because she looked as if she were up to something.

"Now never you mind, and don't pry either. You know your birthday is coming up, and you're so hard to surprise, so don't go snooping," she said as she stood and worked her way around the table to him. She placed her hands gently on each side of his face and gave him a kiss as she said, "I've got to go check on something. I should be back in about an hour."

"Don't I even get a hint?"

"No! And you just leave it right there. No questions," she instructed, waving her index finger at him on her way out the door.

It was a very short drive for Mary Beth as she took the bridge that crossed Clear Creek and cut through the back pasture to their gate on the backside of Clover Town. She was in a hurry. She knew a good deal when she saw one and was not about to pass it up. The directions in the newspaper were perfect, and she was relieved to see there was only one truck in the driveway of the seller's house. She saw an old horse trailer parked on the side of the house, but it was not hooked up to a truck.

"Good. I bet I'm the first one here. It's only eight o'clock in the morning," she said to herself as she stepped from the truck and started toward the front door.

"Can I help you, ma'am?" Clint asked as he peered around the corner of the house, holding two buckets of feed.

"Yes, you can. I am here about the two horses, and I assume from what I read, you are giving them away."

"Yes ma'am, that's correct, but I didn't think that ad would be out 'til tomorrow."

Mary Beth walked over to Clint and extended her hand to introduce herself. He was a horrible sight to see. His eyes were sunken and surrounded by shadows; his skin was almost ash-gray in color. He reeked of liquor, and his clothes were wrinkled. He had on a cowboy hat, but Mary Beth could tell by the way his hair hung down in greasy strands that he had not been taking care of himself. She had a sixth sense about people, and she could tell that Clint was in distress. She observed that he had no wedding ring on his finger nor was there a tan line from the absence of one. His eyes were yellow, and his hand shook ever so slightly as she took it in hers and introduced herself.

"I'm Mary Beth. I hope you don't mind me coming over so early, but it looked like such a great deal, I just had to get here and be the first one to see these horses."

Mary Beth was from a family of horse breeders before she married Bo. She knew her horseflesh, knew what to look for in the shoulders, back, and legs of a fine horse. As she shook Clint's hand, she peered over his shoulder at the two horses in a corral. The mare was breathtaking, a shimmering blanket of brown. Her colt was the same, his chestnut body chiseled with fine lines and long muscle. She sensed immediately that these horses could be worth thousands of dollars.

Clint escorted her to the fence, and they leaned over the top rail as they spoke. He shared the story of his brother and how he came to own the property and the two horses. When she noticed his limp, she inquired as to how he came by it. In short time, they spoke with the ease of good friends.

Through it all, Mary Beth could tell that something was not quite right with this young man; however, she did not pry. Instead, she gracefully enticed the stories from Clint, one after another—about the horses, the property, his family, his life.

A short time later, another truck drove into the driveway. Two men exited the truck and made their way to the back of the house—another response to the ad in the paper. Clint excused himself as he approached the two men. They met him halfway between the front of the house and the fence, where Mary Beth patiently waited. She crossed her fingers and gave silent prayer.

Only moments later, the two men were heading back to their truck, and Clint back to the fence. He smiled at Mary Beth.

"Ma'am, I hope you enjoy them. I have the papers in the house. I'll go get them for you."

"You do know that I'm not going to let you get away with giving me these two horses without paying you for them. They're not some kind of derelict animals you just give away. They're fine horseflesh; as a matter of fact, they are some of the finest horses I've seen in a long time. We will discuss a price, and I'll pay it."

Mary Beth was very firm in her tone, but Clint had other ideas.

"I don't want any money for them, ma'am. They just need a good home. I have no emotional attachment to them; I don't even know their names. I don't have the time or inclination to take care of them. They're much better off with a family who can love them and ride them."

Clint lowered his head, his eyes hidden beneath the brim of his cowboy hat. His voice, though rough and gritty like sandpaper, never cracked, but Mary Beth knew he was suffering. *There is something more to this,* she thought.

Clint decided to kick it up a notch, all the while trying his best to avoid eye contact with his visitor. "You see, ma'am," he said. "I will be heading back out on the rodeo trail shortly, and I can't take care of the horses."

Mary Beth saw clear as glass through his mediocre lies and wondered what he would say if she pressed for his date of departure or other details. Instead, she remained silent.

Clint invited her into the house while he retrieved the papers for the two horses. While she waited in the main room, she marveled at how clean the home was; in fact, it smelled of fresh lemon. She saw no dust or dirt. The kitchen on the far side of the open floor plan was just as neat. No pots and pans were left out. In the rack next to the sink, fresh clean dishes dried in the soft breezes that blew through the open windows. *This home does not match this disheveled man.*

Clint returned with papers in hand, and they sat at the kitchen table. Mary Beth eagerly traced back the bloodline of the mare.

"I knew the lines on the mare looked familiar," she finally said, her excitement palpable. "She is from a bloodline that once belonged to my grandfather. Your brother kept outstanding records, and the colt, Whisky by the Drink, has a bloodline filled with every quality necessary to be a world champion."

"What's that you say? What is the name of the two-year-old?"

"Whisky by the Drink," she repeated, pointing to the name on the papers.

"Well, I'll be." Clint said as he stood and walked into the kitchen. "Ma'am, you must excuse my manners; could I interest you in a cup of coffee?"

Upon hearing the name of the horse, Clint knew that if there ever was a sign, that was it. His brother had named that horse, and the name had meaning. Whisky was what he had loved the most, his best friend, and it had led him to his grave. For the first time in more than a year, something made sense to Clint. And for the first time in more than a year, he wanted coffee more than a whisky.

Clint turned on the coffeemaker at the far corner of the kitchen counter. Within a few minutes, the coffee was trickling down into the glass pot. Mary Beth was going on about how she wanted to purchase the two horses for her husband's birthday and how important it was to train Whisky by the Drink because of his bloodline and potential.

Then she said something that snapped Clint to attention. "... and you'd be the perfect man for the job."

She went on about how the ranch needed someone like Clint to manage the barn and the livestock, reassuring him of the rightness of it all. Mary Beth was in her element; it would be useless for Clint to attempt a rejection of this fine opportunity. She prided herself on being a professional when it came to recognizing when someone was in need. By the time Clint had returned to the table with the two cups of coffee, she'd laid out the entire future of the two horses—with Clint as no small player in the story.

She paused long enough to take a sip of the coffee and give the young cowboy time to try to create an objection. He reminded her of his responsibilities to the rodeo, that he would be moving on, but she took that as seriously as if he'd said he'd grown wings. She began discussing wages, working hours, and even benefits to a trainer of his caliber, for she could see attributes to his accomplishments scattered along the walls and shelves of the house. Clint was stifled and sat quietly.

It was then that she switched gears from horses and business to life.

"Don't let the weeds have it, Clint," she said in a much softer tone than before.

"Beg your pardon, ma'am?"

"Have you ever planted a garden, Clint?" she asked.

"No, ma'am, can't say I have."

"You see, life is like a garden. We place it in not just the best, but the very best spot, where it can bathe in full, radiant sunshine. We feed it only the best—plenty of water along with the perfect mixture of soils and nutrients. Then we diligently fuss over it with constant maintenance, weeding out those things that rob our plants and smother their growth.

"We clear a spot in our hearts for the things we want to grow in our lives," she added gently, "the same as we do for a garden. We plant love, joy, happiness, and all the things that make life worth living. Then we try our best to keep out the bad things, so they don't choke out the good. If you don't constantly tend your life like a garden, the weeds will surely creep in and take over. They are relentless and many. If you let them take over, you will never be able to enjoy the sweet taste of fulfillment that a well-maintained garden, or life, can offer."

Clint drew in a deep, sobering breath as he looked in Mary Beth's direction. Over her shoulder, through the kitchen window, a breeze lightly blew through the drapes. She seemed like an angel to him at that moment. His mind cleared as his subconscious took hold of her words.

"Happiness has a way of catching up to you, if you let it. You know that, don't you, Clint?"

# 16

Clint laughed inwardly, suddenly aware of what had just transpired. He'd been boondoggled! He'd been exposed and now could not hide from this kind woman.

With an open heart, he looked at Mary Beth and said, "I don't know if it is that easy for me. I have always been sort of a loner, but I still want to be around people—just not so much. Does that make sense?"

"Yes, it does. Is that why you stayed with a rodeo so long?"

"Yes, ma'am. The people on the crew understood my ways and became my family. The constant moving from town to town and new faces filled me with excitement. I loved everything about the rodeo, from the dirty laundry right down to the broken bones and crappy pay." He paused and then apologized, "Sorry for my language, ma'am."

She smiled and reassured him that she was no stranger to harsh language.

She stood up, collected both of their coffee cups, and went to the sink. She ran water in both cups, then over her hands as she glanced to the stovetop percolator on the range. It looked much like the stainless steel ones Bo had used on the cattle drives long ago; she figured the bygone-era pot was still functional. Looking back over her shoulder to where he sat at the table, she said, "No offense, but I would love to make us a proper pot of coffee. I'm not saying yours is bad or anything. I'd just like you to try mine. I think you'll like it."

"I'm sure you're right, ma'am. It's been a long time since I've made a cup of coffee, and it never was that good to begin with."

He offered to help, but Mary Beth insisted she be allowed

to do it herself. "It'll give me a chance to snoop around in your cupboards," she said, reminding him that this was something all good women did with or without permission anyway.

Clint nodded his head, then shook it slowly side to side, not sure whether to protest or concede.

"Where is your nutmeg?"

He led her to a neatly stocked shelf of spices. All of the labels faced out, so they could easily be read from allspice to zesty orange peel. She was impressed at the well-stocked kitchen.

"You must like to cook," she replied as she sprinkled the nutmeg into the coffee grinds.

"Yes, ma'am. I find that cooking at the end of the day helps me relax."

She bypassed the automatic coffeemaker on the counter and went to the percolator on the back burner of the stove. She filled the metal pot with water at the sink and placed it on the stove, and then turned up the gas burner to a slow simmer. The flames just short of the bottom of the pot danced like fireflies trapped in a glass bottle. She explained to Clint that coffee brewed on an open flame along with a few pinches of nutmeg created a magical taste.

She then swore him to secrecy, saying, "This is one of the secrets that makes my husband love me so, a little mystery that keeps him guessing. The smile on his face in the morning when he drinks his first cup of coffee makes me as happy as he. So don't you share my secret that is now yours too, and I hope it brings you just as much happiness."

After a few more minutes of light conversation, the coffee was ready. It splashed into the glass knob at the top of the lid, signaling it had perked to perfection. Mary Beth poured a cup for Clint and delivered it to the table, never skipping a beat in her telling of her days on the ranch: how so many of their hired hands had been disappointments, unreliable and unskilled, unable to train a horse if their life depended on it.

As Clint listened, he leaned forward in his chair to retrieve the cup on the table and take a sip. His eyes widened before the liquid hit his lips, the aroma of the coffee gently tickling his senses. His eyes widened further at the taste of it, pleasantly surprised that a cup of coffee could taste so good. Perhaps the company made it so. Either way, clearly both were missing in his life.

Clint became more and more relaxed with this woman, sharing information about his life with ease. Mary Beth had a way of gently knocking down his barriers that he so carefully had constructed against most people. He listened intently as she spoke of her wishes to surprise her husband with the two horses. They were then interrupted by another truck coming down the drive, towing a horse trailer. Clint excused himself as he went outside to greet the visitors, who were likely responding to his ad, to inform them that the horses were spoken for.

As he stepped back into the house, Mary Beth was heading toward him.

"Well, I'll be," she said. Her face was flush, and her hands trembled ever so slightly as she held up the breeder papers for Whisky.

"What is it? Is there something wrong?" Clint asked, perplexed.

"No! In fact everything is right. Perfectly right," she exclaimed as she lowered her reading glasses to the tip of her nose and the paper to the table, holding it with both hands. "Do you believe in serendipity? Because if you do, this was meant to be. You see, Whisky's birthday and my husband's are the same! Well, of course the year is different, but the day is precisely the same. A horse from my grandfather's best bloodline has the same birthday as my husband. And I am here to take that horse home for his birthday."

"Well ma'am, the fact is I don't much believe in fate or such fancy words as serendipity, but in the last hour or so, I am starting to believe in something as simple as good fortune," he said. He started to sit and enjoy some more joe when another truck with a horse trailer started coming up the drive.

Mary Beth stopped him before he could head out the door. "So will you do it?" she asked. "And don't pretend you don't know what I'm talking about. What I'm offering you was meant to be. Whether you like it or not, that horse ties us all together. So don't even think about saying no." Her tone was both excited and matter-of-fact, like she was about to close the biggest deal of her life.

"Well, ma'am, I must admit that the circumstances are quite overwhelming."

Mary Beth waited, smiling, hands resting calmly on the table.

"However," Clint said, "I was willing to say yes at the first sip of your coffee."

A smile as wide as Texas stretched across her face, and it sparkled from cheek to cheek. Her face was alive with the joy of victory on many levels. Not only had she gotten what she came for, she'd rescued someone who needed help but had no idea how to ask for it. She'd found someone to lend a hand to her husband at the ranch and to train the new horses, helping to sew a thread from her past into the Kelso family legacy.

Clint took a long sip of coffee and held the cup in both hands, as if he were caressing a precious gift. He stared into the pool of dark, steamy liquid, breathing in the hint of nutmeg. Closing his eyes, he indulged himself completely in the aroma. He then placed his cup on the table, and turned his full attention to his new friend.

"Ma'am, if you will excuse me, I need to put up a sign at the end of the driveway saying that the horses already have a new home, or I will never get a chance to enjoy your extraordinary coffee in peace."

Peace. Something he had not known in a very long time.

# 17

Yanked from the familiar suburbs of Houston to finish off his 1982-83 junior high school year in the country, Kevin Ferris was fast learning to adjust to the many changes in his young life. Not only had his mom and dad moved him to Pearland, Texas—a small dot of a town that entertained commuters with a single traffic light and snuggled up close to Clover Town—his sister Tammy, who was seven years older, left home to begin college at Louisiana State University.

*The country,* Kevin thought more than once, *is more like the end of the earth and if I take one more step, I'll just fall right off it.*

His new school was not as ethnically diverse as his old one, and it was so far away he had to ride the bus instead of his bicycle. It was as if he had lost all control of his own destiny. At his old school, he was on the swim team and starting to place second and third in some of his events. His coaches even told him he showed natural ability, and if he kept up with his training, colleges would look at him for consideration for scholarships when he reached high school. His new school only offered baseball and football, neither of which he had ever played or wanted to play.

His old school had mostly black and Hispanic students in it, a completely opposite ethnic makeup to his new school. Back in his old school, the division between the student populace was not so much race, but an attitude of toughness. Those kids who could give an air of toughness, and were prepared to fight the good fight if needed, were usually left alone as the bullies sought out softer prey. Kevin, although small for his age and built like a stick—a thin stick—learned very quickly which category he wanted to be in.

Eddie Flowers was Kevin's best friend, and his dad had been a Golden Gloves boxer in the Navy. Mr. Flowers taught the two of them how to hit a speed bag, which was mounted on the wall of their garage, when the boys were nine years old.

"This is a skill every young man should learn," Mr. Flowers had explained. Enthralled, the boys watched as the movement of his hands rhythmically bounced the bag faster and faster.

The speed bag was mounted so high on the wall the boys could not reach it. Even if they jumped as high as they could, they would only touch it with the tips of their fingers. Mr. Flowers had stacked up two apple crates just far enough away from the speed bag to where the boys could stand on top of them and hit it at the proper height. Eddie was the first to stand on the crates, swinging his little fists at the bag.

"I'm going to fall, Dad. Can't we just lower the speed bag?" Eddie had asked.

"If I did that, you wouldn't learn balance at the same time you're swinging your fists. A good punch comes from a balanced position. Once you've learned how to hit the bag and not fall from the crates, I'll teach you how to hit with power. Balance is extremely important, son. If you can't stay on your feet, then you may as well be just another wrestler."

The boys hung on every word Mr. Flowers said. To them, he was as close to a hero as one could get.

"The next lesson I will teach you is how to protect yourself and not get hit at all. Learning good balance is the first important tool in protecting yourself. But the strongest lesson I want you to remember is to never be the kind of person who uses these skills in bad ways, to bully or harm an innocent person." Eddie's father stopped and pointed his finger at the two of them. "Don't become the bully, because if you do, you have missed the whole reason I am teaching you to box."

He turned back to the bag and made one last powerful blow that sounded like thunder. The bag smashed against the backboard several times before it hung down and dangled in small circles. "Gentlemen protect others and themselves and are honorable. Bullies protect nothing and are punks."

Kevin understood immediately and promised to be a faithful student. That afternoon marked his first boxing lesson, one of many that would continue until his family moved away.

Kevin's new junior high school had its own share of bullies that he would again have to navigate. Eddie and he had developed a keen sense of how to avoid trouble: where to sit for lunch, what cliques to steer clear of, that kind of stuff. Now he had to start all over again.

The timing of having to move before the school year ended was also a stressor for Kevin, but apparently unavoidable. Their old house had sold almost immediately after putting it on the market, and his parents found a hot deal on this new house in Pearland. All these things were wonderful for Jane and Allen Ferris—like all the stars had aligned perfectly for them—but it was just the opposite for Kevin. He was lost in the shuffle of his parents' excitement about moving to this fabulous home and "safer" community.

His first day at Pearland Junior High was as bad as he'd expected. The bus was a hassle, as no one wanted to share their seat with him. The classroom seating was similar, though thankfully some of the classes had assigned seating. The lockers were all taken. For the first time in his life, Kevin would have to work his way into the rank structure. If this had been the first day of the school year, he could have merged into the population fairly unnoticed. Instead, he was wheeled into his first class in a giant fish bowl guided by one of the school counselors.

"Everyone, please welcome Kevin Farris. He is new. His family just moved here from Houston," the counselor explained to all the curious onlookers.

Kevin felt as if he were the main attraction at the freak show just outside the circus tents. *Step right up folks. Pay a dollar to see the freak.*

The counselor held firmly onto Kevin's shoulders as she directed him to his seat. *God, please open up the floor and let me fall in so I can hide* was Kevin's silent prayer.

As Kevin and Mrs. Friendly walked to his desk, everyone's eyes followed him in perfect unison, as if they were watching a funeral procession. It took fourteen long steps to reach the desk—he counted—where he could at least hide his nervous shaking. He sat down quickly, noticing for the first time that the boy behind him was a black boy, the only black boy in the classroom, maybe in the whole school as far as he'd seen.

Kevin tried to survey the room with his peripheral vision and not be too conspicuous. At least the desk afforded him some camouflage from the curious students, comfortable in their familiar world and well established in the pecking order. Finally, some relief came in the form of quiet chatter as the teacher allowed the students to discuss a passage they had just finished reading prior to Kevin's glorious arrival.

"Hey, my name is Leonard Parker." The voice came from behind him, and Kevin turned to see a black hand extended in greeting. Kevin shook it.

Before long, Kevin had a good history of Leonard, who knew how to make the most of his minutes. After explaining that, like Kevin, he too had been yanked up from his cozy world in San Antonio to Pearland just a year ago.

"My mom is Lynette Parker, a teacher here at Pearland."

"That's nice."

"Not really," said Leonard matter-of-factly. He then went on to tell more about himself, barely breaking for an occasional "uh-huh" from Kevin, who tried his best to keep up. Leonard's father had been a pilot in the Air Force and died in a plane crash when Leonard was just two years old. His sister Michelle attended Texas A&M University at College Station. His mom finally decided to move herself and Leonard to Pearland to teach at the junior high, to be closer to her relatives, and to get away from the sound of the jets as they flew over their home in San Antonio, which reminded all of them of their late father, whose name was Levi.

Leonard took a breath. Kevin was about to break in with a comment or two of his own, but Leonard started right back up again.

Leonard was of the same mindset that Pearland was like a foreign country. In San Antonio, he had been one of many black students mixed in with a fairly balanced number of whites and Hispanics. Luckily for him, his mother moved them during the summertime. Even though he was one of only six black children in the entire school, starting school with everyone else had made the new school a little less daunting. "It gave me a chance to fit in, instead of feeling like a fish in a big glass bowl."

"You don't say," Kevin said.

Then class was dismissed.

To Kevin's delight, the boys shared three other classes together. This changed everything for Kevin, as the newness became more tolerable. Leonard also seemed happy with his new friend and the situation, which allowed him to show off his scholarly skills and get Kevin caught up on the curriculum.

During lunchtime, they sat together in the cafeteria and shared more information about themselves over sandwiches, apples, a few slices of cheese, and a Coca-Cola from the vending machine. By the end of the day, the two of them had discovered many similarities between themselves and their families. A friendship had begun.

On the bus, they sat together, picking up where they left off during school.

"I saw your parents moving in down the street last week, but I never saw you," Leonard remarked.

"That's because I always had a box in my hands, which covered my face. I didn't see you on the school bus this morning," Kevin said.

"That's because I ride with my mother to work every day. Well, her work—my school, you know what I mean."

"Yeah, I know what you mean. Do you have her for any of your classes?"

"No, thank God. That would be unbearable."

Kevin agreed.

Leonard added, "It wouldn't be a bad thing, to be a student in one of my mother's classes, but it would give other kids the opportunity to pick on me. I would definitely be called the teacher's pet."

Again, Kevin agreed.

"Do you like to fish?" Leonard asked.

Music to Kevin's ears. "I love to fish! I fish a lot with my grandfather and father. We used to have a small boat, but Dad sold it years ago, so now the only fishing I do is when I get to go with some friends of mine. Unfortunately those friends are in Houston and I'm here. Why do you ask?"

"Because your house backs up to a creek, no farther away than the length of your driveway. I figured you knew that already."

"No, I had no idea. I spent all weekend unloading boxes inside the house. I haven't gotten outside to look around yet. Besides that, Dad told me the property behind our house belonged to someone else and I needed permission to go on it."

"I've been back there a few times, and I have seen a man riding a horse. I think he's the rancher that owns the property. He's seen me fishing in the creek but never said anything. He rode by once and kind of waved at me, so I think it's okay. I mean, he didn't run me off or anything like that."

Kevin's eyes grew wide with excitement as he listened to Leonard tell him about his fishing trips on the weekends. More and more, he was feeling good about the move and less anxious about fitting in.

Now all he could think about was fishing. The bus ride home was agonizingly long. There was a paradise just outside his bedroom window, and now that he knew about it, he could hardly wait to explore.

He said goodbye to his new friend and hopped off the bus, feeling much better about life in general. They would meet up again in a few minutes. Leonard lived just down the road, six houses away. Of course, six houses away was still a good bit of distance, since each lot was several acres wide. That was another big difference between the country and living closer to the city. Kevin's old house was a small lot, a bitty patch of grass in the front yard, which met up to a sidewalk and a paved road. There were certainly no horses or livestock around. A push mower and ten minutes of muscle was all that was required in order to manicure the yards, front and back. The homes were so close together, a car couldn't fit between them.

When Kevin heard Leonard's knock at the front door, he raced to answer it. He ushered Leonard through the house to the back porch, and then they headed to the barbed wire fence which separated them from paradise. Not a single thread of their tattered jean cutoffs or T-shirts got caught on the sharp prongs as they slipped through. On the other side of the fence, they stopped for a moment and stared at every boy's dream: hundreds of acres of trees, an enormous stretch of woodlands split down the middle by a shallow creek with steep banks.

They did not bring their fishing poles on their first adventure together, but they did bring their imagination and energy. They ran through the woods down as many trails as possible, touching every leaf along its edges. They stopped at the beginning of one of the clearings and climbed an enormous live oak. As they stood on the arms of its massive branches, high in the canopy, they saw before them small ponds dotting the fertile green pastures. They speculated on how many fish and what kind and how big they were, vowing to catch them all. As far as the eye could see in every direction there was only nature, green trees and bushes, carpets of grasses, and flowers of all colors. They inhaled the air, fragrant and clean, relishing every inch of it. They scanned the horizon, planning future days in the sunshine.

Once again, they felt in control of their destinies now that they had each other and this, this beautiful land to explore together.

Finally, Leonard and Kevin headed home, knowing their parents would be home soon and there were chores to do before dinner. They passed back through the barbed wire fence reluctantly, for they didn't want to leave, but filled with hope for the future.

# 18

"Kevin?" Allen Ferris looked at his son with raised brows, holding up a muddy pair of tennis shoes that Kevin had left on the back porch. "Is there a mud hole somewhere in the yard that I don't know about?"

"No, Dad. They got muddy when I went through the creek."

"You mean the creek on the backside of the property, the same creek on the other side of the fence?"

"Yes sir, but it's okay for me to go back there. I was with my new friend down the street. His name is Leonard, and he and I have four classes together in school. He said it's okay if we play back there, that the rancher doesn't mind. You should see it, Dad! The whole place is loaded with trees and little ponds and so many places to fish, it would take forever."

"Well, just because your friend down the street has permission to go back there and play doesn't mean you have permission to go back there and play too. You need to speak to the rancher yourself and make sure it's okay that you play back there, and your friend should do the same if he hasn't yet."

"New friend?" Jane Ferris appeared in the room with an armful of groceries. "When do we get to meet your new friend?"

"Oh, Mom, you will love him," Kevin said. "His mother is a teacher at our school, and he just moved here from somewhere else too. Well, about a year ago."

The questioning went on for several minutes as Kevin and his parents exchanged stories about their days, with most of the focus on Kevin's first day at his new school. As they talked, several trips were made back and forth between his mother's car and the kitchen.

Allen and Jane were immensely happy that their son had what seemed to be a good first day and had already made a friend. They were concerned, however, about the boys strolling through the ranch property uninvited, and they insisted again on the boys obtaining permission to be on it. The rancher's name was well-known to the community—a Mr. Kelso. Jane and Allen had learned about him from the realtor.

Jane belabored the point to Kevin some more, even though he'd already heard it from his father. "I know your friend has permission, so you say, but you'll have to check with Mr. Kelso himself. We are new here, and I don't want any problems. So after dinner, you and your father can drive over and speak to him."

Kevin just rolled his eyes and exhaled as he dropped his shoulders. "Geez, mom, you always have to make such a big deal out of everything." He pivoted on one foot as he half-turned to walk away.

"It is a big deal, and you know it's the right thing to do. How would you like it if you came home and the rancher was sitting on our front porch, letting his horse graze on our beautiful yard?"

"Now how would he do that, Mom? There is no gate for the horse to walk through on the back of our property."

"You get my point. You either ask permission or you don't get to go back there at all—your choice."

Kevin looked over his mother's shoulder at his father, who was nodding his head with his arms crossed, and Kevin knew it would be done just the way Mom wanted it done—only he wanted to do it with Leonard.

"Okay, okay. But I'll go tomorrow with Leonard, so the rancher can meet both of us."

"Great idea, son," said Allen as he mussed Kevin's hair, which he knew Kevin hated.

# 19

The following morning, Kevin waited at the end of his shell driveway for the school bus, clutching his lunchbox, a few books, and a yellow notepad. The dread he'd felt the day before had lifted just a little. He'd made a new friend and was looking forward to the end of the day when he and Leonard could explore the ranch and surrounding properties. This time, they already planned to take their fishing poles to try their luck in one of the small ponds, which Leonard called Cattle Tank Pond.

The bus lumbered up the road and squealed to a slow stop, double doors swinging wide open. Kevin reached up for the handle and pulled his way up the stairs and into the aisle. The seats were the typical arrangement for school buses, designed for maximum capacity and high utility. Scanning for an open place to sit, Kevin heard the welcome sound of Leonard's voice calling to him. "Kevin, back here. I saved you a spot."

Kevin's frown of concentration melted away as he staggered down the aisle of the accelerating bus, grabbing on and leaning into the bench seats, making his way to Leonard's seat near the back of the bus. Exchanging hellos, Kevin flopped into the seat.

"I thought you rode with your mother in the morning," Kevin asked with surprise.

Leonard gave a little nod. "Yeah, I decided that today I would ride the bus so we can hang out together. The best part is the bus stops at my house before it runs back around the street, so I can save us a seat."

Kevin was relieved, because his first ride on the bus yesterday was a little tense. No one seemed to want him on the bus; however, Kevin knew that was the norm for kids his age. No one knew his status, where he fit in, or whom he hung out with; these were all important questions that needed answering before anyone would take a chance on letting a new kid into any circles, or even a conversation. Status was a big deal among adolescents.

As soon as some of the kids saw him talking to Leonard—who had already negotiated his way through this same process over the summer—more kids were willing to engage him. Leonard was well-liked by the other kids, and by default, that extended to Kevin somewhat. He just wished more junior high kids lived on his street, which seemed to be overgrown with grade-schoolers. The fifteen or so middle-schoolers all lived on the streets before Kevin's house, which was basically the last stop on the way into school. By the time the bus dropped off the grade-schoolers and made its way to the junior high school, Leonard had introduced Kevin to everyone on the bus. It really helped knock off the edge of anxiety that loomed over Kevin's first few days of school.

"Thanks, man," Kevin said. He hopped off the bus step to the ground, and Leonard did the same. They started walking to their first class, which they had together.

"For what?" Leonard asked.

"For riding the bus and saving me a seat, helping me break the ice. I mean, you could have ridden with your mom."

Leonard gave Kevin a friendly slap in the middle of his back as they walked.

"Oh no, thank *you*," Leonard explained. "Because of you, I now have a good excuse not to ride with my mom. She likes to sing to the radio at the top of her lungs while we are driving, and she always makes me join in. Plus I have to wake up thirty minutes earlier because she has meetings in the mornings. I would much rather ride the bus with you. Mom is a morning person and far too cheerful and happy. I like it quiet in the mornings. I told her that you needed me to show you around."

*That's a little strange*, Kevin thought. He would much rather ride to school with his mom or ride his bike, like he did back in Houston. However, Pearland Junior High was a good eight miles from his new house, so he had no choice.

"Besides that, if I ride home with my mom, I sometimes get stuck waiting for her in the library for an extra forty-five minutes because of teachers' conferences, and that, my friend, is time the two of us could spend fishing."

A rush of excitement came over both boys, and they almost ran to their first class as if it would somehow speed up the time. It would be a long day for Kevin and Leonard.

The bus flipped routes on the way back, so Kevin was dropped off first at his driveway. Just before the bus doors flapped opened, Leonard hollered that he would be right down once he picked up his fishing gear. Kevin gave a thumbs-up and hopped down the stairs, happy to have an after-school plan. It was a school night and both boys had homework; however, it would be almost an hour before either of their parents got home. To the boys, the expedition was as necessary and important as cramming knowledge into their heads, which they had done plenty.

As the bus sped away down the gravel road, it left the familiar cloud of swelling dust to float over the yard before it settled. In a hurry, Kevin bolted to the front door, vaguely noticing the ten or so empty boxes tossed on the lawn. He barely turned the doorknob when his mother flung open the front door as wide as she could.

"Hi, honey. How was your second day at school?" she blurted out, smiling with enthusiasm. She reached out and pulled him through the front door and into her arms, squeezing him hard. His books and lunchbox were still in his arms, now pinned against his sides as his mom danced him around with her enormous hug.

"It was fine, Mom," he managed to vocalize. "You're smothering me." His nose and lips were smashed and contorted against her neck.

Finally releasing him, she wiped beads of sweat from her

forehead. She was dressed in shorts and one of his father's white T-shirts, balled up in a large knot at the front to take up the slack material. Her hair, which usually was fashionably styled, was stuck up in a wild bun on the top of her head. Her feet were bare.

Kevin knew this manner of dress very well—housework attire—and she was at it hard. Unfortunately, when his mom was working, she expected "all hands on deck" to be working too. The worst was that she usually planned these grand events—like gardening or housecleaning—in the mornings: no sleeping in. The last conversation he'd had with his sister, just before she went away to college, was about this very thing. She'd rubbed his head and said with mock pity, "Sorry to leave you here by yourself; hopefully, you'll survive." He knew exactly what she meant—boy, did he know.

His father was the smart one. He always had a good excuse lined up—just in case—so he could make his escape. Once Kevin caught him telling a friend to ring him back in five minutes. When his friend called, his dad acted out an elaborate, animated crisis in detail, saying he had to go help his buddy and that he would be right back. Sure, he'd come back, but only after the chores were done. Mom was good at ambushing the three of them. Dad and his acting skills allowed him an escape or two. Kevin's sister went to college to escape. And Kevin was stuck holding the broom.

"I thought you were at work."

"I got off early so I could unpack more boxes, and now that you're home, you can help. Isn't that great?" She stood with her arms extended wide, smiling, head cocked to one side, eyes wide and bright. She looked like a mom gone mad.

She said, "Now put down your books and give me a real hug."

Kevin opened his arms, dropping everything straight to the floor, and walked forward, taking short, choppy steps like a zombie. He hung his head low, so far down that his chin touched his chest, and he let all the air from his lungs as he said, "Oh, okay" in that same flat, monotone voice as before. His mom was a hugger, and a squeezer, and a rocker, a deadly embarrassing combination. She insisted on full-body hugs too. That meant the hug-ee *had* to wrap his or her arms around her and endure the moment. No one was immune. "Okay, Mom," Kevin said again in a muffled voice.

"You are getting so tall."

*Oh no*, Kevin thought, *she is setting me up for something big by sprinkling the sugar on.*

"And strong too."

*Here it comes, she is about to drop the other shoe.*

"And it's a good thing too, so pick up your books and put them away."

Kevin was already plotting an escape. *I will pull a Dad— maybe say I have to get right on my homework.* Then he shook his head, arguing with himself. *No, that won't work. Any minute Leonard will be here with his fishing gear, and she'll know what I'm up to.* He continued to muddle through his options as quickly as possible.

Kevin didn't make a habit of lying to his mother or father— he just wasn't comfortable doing that. He knew plenty of other kids who did, but it seemed that the lying only got them into more trouble than it was worth. He'd also known plenty of parents, and as parents go, his were the absolute best. So he decided to just spit it out, truth and all.

"Mom, I was going to go fishing with Leonard. He will be here any second."

"Kevin," his mom started, "there's far too much work that needs to be done around here."

"Mom!" Kevin begged. "I will only be gone for about an hour. Please." He tried his best whiny-but-still-adorable voice.

She turned to him, placed her hands on each side of his face, and in the same whining voice, mimicked, "But *Mooooooooooom.*" She twisted his cheeks and rocked his head from side to side. But she would not be swayed. "When this house is unpacked, everything is put away, and you get permission from the rancher. Remember we talked about this."

"Okay," Kevin answered, defeated.

"Besides all that, you've got homework, and—this is the most important *why not* of all—I am the only one that knows in which of these multitude of boxes your fishing gear is packed."

"Mom!" Kevin cried out, after several seconds of agony. He dropped his arms and shoulders, as if the weight of them were unbearable, and began a slow, dragging march to his bedroom. His mother placed her hands on his shoulders and joined him step for step all the way to his door. The floor of his room was covered with boxes all marked "Kevin's Room" in bold black marker. He fell onto his bed face first, landing on the only space that was not covered with boxes.

"Mom, I don't want to unpack."

"I know you don't, but I will make a deal with you."

Kevin perked up a little and rolled over on his back. The boxes around him shook and bounced as he flipped over; his legs dangled over the edge of the bed, feet almost touching the floor. His mom was always making deals in order to entice him to do things he was reluctant to do. The good part was they weren't bad deals, and she always made good on her promises— an admirable quality even from a youth's perspective.

"Today is Tuesday," she started. She removed the box from the corner of the bed, leaving a space just large enough for her to sit, and placed it on the floor. "If you help me unpack every day this week after school up to Thursday . . ." She reached over and hoisted him upright, then pulled him over onto her lap and wrapped her left arm around him. He lay as limp and lifeless as a rag doll. ". . . and get permission from the rancher, like we agreed . . ." She elevated her voice to emphasize the point.

"... I will tell you where your fishing gear is, and you and your friend can go fishing all day on Friday."

Kevin lit up with excitement and gave his mom a double-arm hug, shouting, "Thank you, Mom!" Then he stopped abruptly. "Friday is a school day; you mean I can fish after school, right?"

"No," she replied as she walked toward his bedroom door. "Friday is a teacher's workday, so it is a day off for you. Aren't you glad your mom is so smart?" She smirked as she disappeared down the hallway.

Kevin leaped from his bed, jubilant, and started to work on the boxes. He had barely opened the top of the first box when someone knocked at the front door.

"That must be Leonard, Mom. I'll get it."

Kevin ran for the door in order to give Leonard the bad news in person. His mother suddenly stepped from the kitchen and headed for the door in a short, choppy run, swinging her arms and pumping her fists as if she were running a race. "Ha, beat ya," she said as she reached for the door and turned the knob.

*Oh no!* Kevin gasped. *I should have warned Leonard that my mother is a hug fanatic.*

She opened the door wide enough to almost bang the knob into the sheetrock if it hadn't been protected by the doorstop. There stood Leonard, holding all his fishing gear and smiling.

*Here it comes.* Kevin winced in sympathetic facial contortions.

"Hello, you must be Leonard," she said. "I'm Jane Ferris."

Leonard had no clue what was coming. He just smiled even wider with bright eyes as he lifted his brows. "Yes ma'am, it's a pleasure to meet you." Leonard shifted his small, green tackle box to the same arm that held the fishing pole and reached out for Kevin's mom's hand. He gave it a single pump and released it. She then invited him in, apologizing for the stacks of boxes and scattered packing paper. Leonard leaned his rod and tackle box against the porch wall and stepped through the door.

That was when the attack finally came, though mild. Jane

threw an arm over Leonard's shoulder. "We are so glad you are here!" Leonard beamed up at her. Then she pulled him around and gave him the Jane Ferris squeeze.

"Well I'm sure that the two of you want to talk," she sang, retreating through the kitchen door.

"Your mom sure is friendly," Leonard said to Kevin in a low voice.

"It could have been much worse."

As they headed down the hallway to his room, Kevin explained to Leonard the deal he'd just made with his mother. He then looked at all the boxes with something close to dread.

"Man, I'll never get out of here. There are so many boxes, so much stuff. I didn't even know we had all this junk."

"Not a problem," Leonard said matter-of-factly. "I'll help you, and we will get it done much faster."

"Are you sure?"

"Yeah. That's what friends do, right?"

"Right!" And with that, they tore into the task at hand.

Several minutes had passed before Jane poked her head in the door to investigate the goings-on. She found the boys industriously working away.

"Mom, I need some nails so I can hang my pictures on the wall."

"I have them in the living room on the coffee table."

Leonard politely said he would get them and hopped into the hallway.

"Leonard said he would help me every day after school this week so we can go fishing on Friday," Kevin said.

Jane smiled. "That's a good friend," she said, then in a softer voice, "I didn't know he was a black boy. You should have said something." Her tone wasn't angry, more like curious.

Mom didn't like any elephants in the room, to use a phrase he'd learned at school. Before he could respond with anything helpful, Leonard reappeared with nails in hand, and Jane left the room. Within an hour, they had all the boxes in the bedroom completely unpacked. The empty boxes were piled up in the backyard so they could be flattened and consolidated into a pile at the back of the fence to be burned.

During the unpacking process, Kevin's dad had returned home from work. He'd been excited to meet Leonard, giving him a friendly handshake along with a pat on the shoulder.

"I want to thank you for helping Kevin get off to a good start at his new school," he said. "It is nice for him to make a friend on his first day."

His dad listened to their plans with great enthusiasm. Kevin wondered if his dad was surprised at the color of Leonard's skin like his mom had been. This realization came unexpectedly to Kevin. Clearly Leonard was a true friend, who had helped smooth his adjustment to his new surroundings and who even had helped with the chores of unpacking the boxes. It had not even occurred to Kevin that his parents would react negatively to Leonard at all, given the circumstances.

Now, based on his mother's reaction, Kevin was already thinking in terms of "Leonard is my black friend," not just "Leonard is my friend." And he didn't like the way that felt.

Kevin was being very honest with himself. To him it did not make any difference what color his friend was. It had no bearing on their relationship. He rehearsed these points in his mind because he wanted to be ready when he talked to his mom. He wanted to understand why knowing Leonard was a colored boy ahead of time would have made a difference.

At five fifteen, Leonard excused himself to return to his house to finish up homework, but he promised to return tomorrow and help.

"I'll see you in the morning on the bus. I'll save you a seat," Leonard said to Kevin as he headed for the front door.

Kevin's father quickly stuck out a hand and shook Leonard's, thanking him again. Leonard then turned to Kevin's mom, who gave Leonard a quick half-hug, thanking him as well. After Leonard had picked up his pole and box and headed up the road, Kevin's dad said, "You got yourself a good friend, son. I can't think of very many kids who would hang around and help strangers unpack, give up doing what they wanted, such as fishing in this case, in order to help a friend with chores."

"Thanks, Dad," Kevin said, grateful for the confirmation. Out of the corner of his eye, he watched his mom, who had just closed and locked the front door. She leaned backward to stretch her back muscles.

"Mom?" Kevin said.

"I'm so tired, son. What is it?"

Their family was always very open and respectful to each other. They talked about everything, no holds barred. The family motto was, *If you're old enough to ask, you're old enough for the truth.* And Kevin was prepared to know more.

"Why did it matter so much that Leonard was black?"

Jane stopped with her hands on her hips and said, "It doesn't matter at all, I guess. I was just surprised. Would've liked to have known what to expect. That's all." She made her way to the bedroom, and Kevin followed close behind her. His father joined the procession.

"But why does it matter?"

Jane stood at her bedroom door, but Kevin passed right by her and plopped down on the mattress. Without a word, his father did the same.

"Is this going to be something I need to get involved in?" Allen asked speculatively.

"Yes," Kevin said.

"No," Jane followed.

"I hope this doesn't take long. I am as hungry as a bear." Allen lay on his side, propped up on an elbow. "What is this all about?"

"Mom said I should have told her that Leonard was black before he came over," Kevin explained. "I don't understand why that was important. I just didn't even think about it. And I felt bad when Mom said that to me."

Jane sat next to Kevin and put her arm around him. "Kevin, I'm sorry. I was surprised, that's all. I felt caught off-guard."

"But you hugged him. He even said how friendly you were!"

"I know, and he's a dear boy," she said, but her brow furrowed as she thought of something else.

The room was quiet. Jane then dropped her shoulders and sighed heavily. Kevin knew she was about to say something of importance.

She reached out to Kevin, grabbing his hands and pulling him close. Then she looked at Allen and held out a hand to him as well. He held it.

"Mom, are you okay?" Kevin asked.

"I've got to get this right, son." She paused once more, then added, "I am so proud of the way you make friends, in spite of a person's differences."

"You mean like Leonard being black?"

"Yes, and I know that sounds racist, but it is not meant to sound that way. You see, when I was a young girl, black people were kept segregated from white people. When your father and I were young, that's just the way it was. And unfortunately, that's the way our parents taught us to be, and how our parents' parents taught them. I know now that those teachings were wrong, horribly wrong, even though at the time, this was completely normal and accepted by most. But ultimately, it was just plain wrong. But the laws changed faster than the people's opinions."

Allen nodded in agreement as she spoke. Kevin listened closely and did not interrupt.

Jane continued. "I have never had a black friend or even a black neighbor, for that matter. Some of the teachings of my parents still hang with me, I guess. When I saw Leonard for the first time, I was so happy to meet your friend and just wasn't expecting . . ." She sighed deeply. "It absolutely doesn't matter, the color of his skin, Kevin. It's the fact that he is a loyal and fun friend to you, that's all that matters. Honestly, that's all that matters. Forgive me for making you think otherwise even for a minute."

"It's okay, Mom," Kevin said and snuggled in closer.

She said, "Thanks. Leonard is a lovely boy with a playful smile, and he is so polite. I can see why you like him. The truth is, Kevin, you didn't think to mention anything about Leonard being black is because it isn't a factor for you; you are blind to the color of his skin. The friendship already transcends the issues of skin color. And that, my son, makes me want to burst with pride."

Allen added, "Even though I didn't blink an eye on the outside, like your mother, I was taken aback a little myself. It's not a reflection on Leonard; it's a reflection on us. Nothing for you to give another worry about because it won't come up again, I suspect."

Jane nodded her head emphatically. "Oh, I agree completely."

Kevin then locked his arms around his mom, giving her the Jane Ferris squeeze.

# 20

Leonard, true to his word, got off the bus at Kevin's house every day after school and helped him not only unpack boxes, but also catch up with his schoolwork. In Kevin's eyes, Leonard was a genius who never had to study. He was not smart in just one subject; he made top grades in every subject. Leonard was also the fastest book reader Kevin had ever seen.

The first day they'd met, Leonard had a thick, red paperback tucked in his back pocket; the next day, it was replaced with another. Kevin figured that first book had been at least three hundred pages. Finally, Kevin asked, "Did you read that other book already?"

"Yeah, I like to read. If you ever want to borrow one, let me know. I have stacks of them in my room, but now mostly I just check them out from the library. I read so many so fast that it's cheaper that way."

Kevin screwed up his face in disgust. "You've got to be kidding me. I hate to read. When I have to write a book report, I just about lose my mind thinking about all the reading."

"Don't worry. I'll help you out. Plus, it'll give me a reason to read another book."

Kevin could only respond with a bewildered look.

———◆———

Normally, Kevin was only allowed to have people in the house if his parents were home. However, in Leonard's case, Kevin was riding a wave of good fortune with all the guilt floating around the house lately. First, Kevin knew his parents felt guilty about moving him away from the only home he'd ever known, right at the same time his sister had gone to college. Second, he knew they felt bad about taking him from his swim team and friends. Last, he felt certain there was some residual guilt about their conversation after Leonard's first visit. Adding in the fact that Leonard was so helpful at the house and was fast becoming the best friend Kevin had ever had, Leonard was a shoo-in for "exception to the rule." Life was good for Kevin Ferris.

Not only had the boys bonded but so had the parents. Leonard's mother Lynette quickly befriended Jane and Allen, and they looked to each other for assistance with the boys and scheduling. Lynette would check in on the boys after school, even if it were only for a brief moment. Allen and Jane in turn helped Lynette balance the many demands of single motherhood. And to show their appreciation for their newfound friends, Allen and Jane planned a grand Sunday feast at the Ferris household. It was to be their first official celebration in their new house.

Sundays and Sunday dinners were a big deal to Kevin's parents, though Kevin didn't feel the same way. To him, the day was far too filled with schedules and things to do that weren't on *his* list of things to do. To make matters worse, Sunday weather always seemed to be tauntingly sunny and mild, just calling him to come outside and be free.

Out of bed by eight, cleaned up and dressed by ten, followed by a sit-down breakfast, church in Houston, and back home by two—or possibly even later, depending on whatever volunteer work his mother might have signed them up for. Once home, everyone would change into more casual attire, but not the kind he could play in. After that, it was often off to dinner at someone's house or entertaining at theirs. Admittedly, he liked it better when his mom and dad entertained church members at home, because then he could always sneak off to his room and avoid the social jousting among the adults. For whatever reason, he always seemed to be the only kid his age at all these gatherings.

This particular Sunday was going to be completely different than the usual grind, though, and Kevin was impatient for it to begin. With a little luck, he might talk his parents into letting him and Leonard go fishing instead of hanging around the edges of adult after-dinner conversations. In the meantime, he set his sights on Friday.

It was the longest week either of the boys could remember. They anticipated the end of the week with such vigor that they lost sleep, tossing and turning all night. In fact, Leonard spent the night at Kevin's on Thursday, just so they could be closer to the barbed wire fence when the morning sun produced enough light for them to see.

But, like any plan laid on a foundation of excitement and youth, Kevin and Leonard's plan had a few flaws.

Friday mercifully arrived, coming off another night of high anticipation and sleeplessness. Mom came in at precisely eight twenty-four a.m.—Kevin hazily could see the numbers on his clock—and reminded him to lock the door behind her when she left for work. Of course, he was so zonked at that point, he didn't move to follow through with the instructions.

———————•————

"Leonard, get up! It's almost nine o'clock!" Kevin yelled in a fit, jumping straight up off the mattress at the realization they'd overslept. Leonard popped his head out from underneath his pillow, eyes wide. He too sprung to his feet. Both boys frantically bounced around the room as they pulled on their clothes and gathered up their fishing gear. They decided to forgo the toothbrush, comb, and face-washing—not important for the day's purposes. They did spend a minute to hastily make up their beds.

Groggy but full of steam, the boys did not dwell on the fact that they had not yet gotten *formal* permission to go on the ranch property. They'd intended to do so, but they'd just never got around to it. So last night, when Allen Ferris asked the boys if they had taken care of the permission agenda, they said that they had—Leonard, while on one of his past fishing excursions, had been okayed to fish there by the rancher. Satisfied that this important matter had been addressed, it did not come up for discussion again.

The boys justified it in their minds: after all, one could construe the rancher's tipping of his hat in Leonard's direction as a sign of acceptance. The rancher had not run him off, so the okay had been given by default. That day, in his youthful exuberance, Leonard just went back to basking in the sun, fishing the day away, without any intervention by the rancher.

Plus, the boys reasoned further, it didn't seem like the rancher cared to talk anyway. He always rode the fence line behind the houses early each morning, just after Kevin and Leonard's parents left for work. Chances were no one from his family or the rancher's were likely to cross paths. The boys thought about maybe being on the safe side and walking to the ranch house, making a proper introduction, and getting formal permission. *But what if he said no? Why chance it?*

Jumping from the back porch, they cleared the three wooden steps down to the grass. After twenty-five or so strides, their foot race ended at the barbed wire fence. Leonard got there first and started passing his rod and reel and then his tackle box through. Kevin did the same. Leonard placed his tennis shoe on the bottom wire and held up the strand above it in order for Kevin to snake his body to the other side without a poke of the barbs.

"Oh darn it!" Kevin remarked, body halfway through the fence. "I forgot to lock the back door."

"Hurry, hurry, hurry," Leonard said.

Kevin quickly ran back to the house. He knew exactly where his key was. This would be lickety-split, in and out, and back to the fence. The key was attached to a small, silver, ball-link chain, like the army dog tag necklaces, and it should've been sprawled across his desk like usual. As he flung open the door, he noticed the brown paper sack with a note attached to it lying on top of the key. His mother had packed a lunch for the two of them along with two water bottles. Kevin came to a quick stop and snapped the note off the bag. His heart raced from the running as he read his mother's words: "You boys have a great day; you've earned it. Love you both, Mom."

He stuffed the note inside the bag, locked the doors, and resumed his race to the back fence. He easily shot through the wire that Leonard held apart for him, as if it was not even there. They grabbed their gear, and without a word, took off across the pasture.

———•———

Bo's morning ride had turned into a slow morning stroll for the both of them. He dismounted Whisky and looped the reins over the saddle horn, setting Whisky free to roam at his side. A cowboy couldn't do that with every horse, but with Whisky, Bo was not worried. He knew that even if his best horse—and best friend—was spooked, he would not leave Bo's side.

The Thoroughbred followed just a few steps behind, stopping occasionally to pluck fresh, dew-covered clover and long-stemmed grasses crowned with flowers, which dangled from his mouth and danced with each rhythmic crunch of his jaw. Every now and again, Bo paused to take in the view of his rolling pastures and heavily wooded ridges that ran along the side of Clear Creek. Sometimes he would find a wire nail that needed pounding to tighten up the fence. Whisky, always the helper, would position himself close enough to Bo so that Bo could retrieve the right tool from the well-equipped saddlebag. The two of them had the repetitive task down to an art form, requiring no hand signals or verbal cues. And when Bo tugged on the fence, the horse knew he would soon receive a "thanks old boy" and a stroke of his neck under his long, brown mane for his efforts. Whisky responded to his touch with flickering eyelashes and a slow nod of his head, leaning into Bo's hand. The bond between the two of them transcended the lines between life and death. His sweet Mary Beth was never far from his thoughts with Whisky at his side, waiting for his time to pass so that he could be with her again.

As far as Bo was concerned, he had done all the things a man was supposed to do. He had learned a trade that supported his family and had shared that knowledge with others. He had raised two respectful, productive children and  kissed the faces of his grandchildren as often as he could, indulging their every wish in an attempt to spoil them the way he wished his grandfather would have spoiled him. He had been a good son to his mother and father, caring for them in their later years and honoring their memories at the gravesite. And most recently, he had weathered the sorrow of burying the only woman he ever loved. His only comfort was the thought that she wouldn't have to bear the same burdens in his death or her children's. All that was left for Bo was to pass the time between now and his last ride along the miles of fence and memories.

Except for that one thing, of course. There was one last task nagging at him to be done, poking at the peace in his soul. The problem was he could not bring himself to the point of actually doing it. It was the shame, stifling to the point of debilitating. In fact, he had come close to giving in to the thought of taking this shame with him to the grave.

Back atop his horse, Bo stopped at the end of the trail that broke through the edge of the woods, giving way to the grand openness of the main pasture. Through it, Clear Creek and its rippling waters flowed to the far boundaries of the property. There, where the water faded into the wood line, Bo caught a glimpse of movement near the woods toward the back pasture. Whisky perked up his ears and raised his head high as he turned his tall shoulders in the same direction Bo was looking. The horse oriented his ears like a radar and lightly stomped the ground with his right front hoof. His short, barely audible snort incited Bo's reaction to the situation.

"Trespassers!" Bo said in a conspiratorial whisper. "Come on, old man. Let's go run them off."

Whisky rotated one ear toward Bo, who leaned forward slightly in the saddle and rubbed the horse's neck in reward for his observation. Whisky's other ear stayed pointed in the direction of the trespassers, as if it were a needle on a compass never varying from true north.

The task of watching for trespassers was something he and Whisky had done many times with all the new development around the ranch. It was actually a welcome distraction, one that took his mind off missing Mary Beth and kept boredom from creeping in. Just hanging around the house sometimes could be torturous with all its physical and emotional reminders: pictures on the walls; her piano, silent, in the parlor; her clothes still in the closet; her unfinished needlepoint in her sewing basket, next to her chair, next to his. They were all good memories that brought him joy and sadness at the same time. Now those distractions came in the form of two youths at the creek of his property.

Bo clicked his tongue against the roof of his mouth and slightly laid out the reins, asking Whisky to walk. They closed the distance between themselves and the boys at a slow but steady pace, the cowboy way: no rush, no panic, just calm and cool. When they arrived at the intruder's entrance point at the woods line, the boys were nowhere in sight. Perhaps the boys had seen him on his horse and had high-tailed it back across the barbed wire fence into the subdivision that bordered the property line.

"That's okay, old man," Bo said as he peered one last time through the trees. "We've done our job. They're gone." With that, he tugged Whisky's reins to the left, in order to turn him toward the barn; however, the horse did not readily respond. Bo combined the rein command with a gentle, right leg command — to no avail. Whisky stood fast, his head and both ears pointed toward the creek bed, into the wooded area beyond, and up the steep bank on the far side of Clear Creek.

"So, they're on the other side of the creek."

Whisky's ears did not move. The horse did not even crank one ear around in Bo's direction for further discussion.

"Okay, I get it," Bo said in a low voice. "But we're not going down that creek bank; you and I aren't as spry as we used to be. Let's go around to the bridge."

When Whisky heard the word "bridge," he turned both ears toward Bo and made a left turn on his own. The bridge was just a few hundred yards from the barn and just wide enough to drive a truck across. Bo's grandfather had built it back in 1866. At the time, it was the only way across Clear Creek for ten miles in both directions. It stretched from the top of the bank on the ranch side to the back pasture side more than eighty yards across. It was about fifty feet high at the tallest point. Over the years, it had been strengthened, made wider, rebuilt, and replaced. The tests of time had taken their toll on the old bridge, as the creek floods turned to vicious torrents, powerful and deadly enough to wash away every weak structure in its path. More than once, the creek had unleashed its fury on the bridge.

Bo let loose of the reins as Whisky walked along the ridgeline trail above the creek. He reached into his saddlebag and retrieved a canteen of water, twisted off the lid, and started to drink.

"You know, we don't have to do this." Whisky turned one ear slightly in Bo's direction. "We may as well go home." Whisky ignored him and kept his pace. "You want some water?" He rattled the canteen so the lid made a clanking sound against its side; still Whisky ignored him and kept walking.

"You'll turn," Bo said, referring to the fact that the bridge was between the two of them and the barn. Most times when a horse is turned toward the barn they won't go past it, because the barn is exactly where they want to be—especially a horse like Whisky. Each time Whisky returned to the barn, he was brushed off by Clint, received his second slice of apple, and was turned out to pasture after cooling down, conveniently tied up to the hitching post next to the cool water trough. It was the royal treatment for a retired Texas cutting horse. "You'll turn," he repeated.

And Whisky did turn: hard right onto the bridge. Bo saw Clint standing just inside the barn, witnessing the old ranch soldiers crossing the bridge. Looking back over his shoulder, Bo gave a shrug, one hand turned palm up. *Who knows?*

———•———

Matt emerged from the barn just behind Clint. All the work for the day was done except preparing Whisky for the pasture. Not the most dedicated ranch hand, Matt was already scoffing. A longer ride meant a longer day to him. Clint, on the other hand, did not care either way; he was happy to find something to do for the wait.

"Where are they going?" Matt asked.

"Don't know."

"Why didn't they come in?"

Clint was silent as he turned back into the barn.

"But! But," Matt blurted out, "how long are they going to be?"

"They'll be back when they're finished," Clint replied.

"Finished with what?"

"And you're not finished."

"Finished with what?" Matt was clearly agitated at this point.

"Finished raking out the goat pen."

"That's greenhorn work," Matt said in a disgusted tone.

"No, it's your work now. You ran off the last two greenhorns because you rode them too hard. Bo should have fired you for that. I swear, I don't know why he keeps you around. Now, you tend to the goats. Carry the goats' water too."

The goats didn't really need tending to, and Clint knew Matt hated doing it, constantly complaining about the smell. Funny thing was the goats liked Matt. They always stayed right beside him, nibbling at his pant legs and following him closely any time he entered the pen. Clint turned the opposite way so he could let loose a full grin as Matt stomped off in the direction of his browsing fans.

———•———

"Okay, if you want to do this, you're on your own. Don't expect any help from me, because I am ready to call it a day," Bo said.

Whisky didn't appear to be listening, deftly stepping off the bridge and turning for the trail that led into the woods.

"Do you know where you're going? You know it would be a lot faster if you took the ridgeline along the creek."

Whisky snorted loudly and flipped his tail hard so the long hairs hit Bo on his left leg.

"Well, you don't have to get all riled up; I was just making a suggestion," Bo said, grinning in appreciation of Whisky's headstrong nature.

The ride continued through the tall pines and winding cattle trails until it let out at the edge of the back pasture. There, sitting on the bank of one of the many small ponds that dotted the landscape, were the two boys. They were shirtless, and each held a fishing pole in one hand and a half-eaten sandwich in the other. They were laughing with abandon at their inner circle of jokes, rocking back and forth, bumping shoulders, and tossing their heads back in response to each other's antics. Their hooting echoed off the trees as if the forest were alive with their contagious joy.

Whisky stopped just out of sight of the boys. The air was still and warm, a precursor to the heat that would surely come at high noon, sending both livestock and cowboy to seek out refuge: the cool shade of willow branches overhanging the creek bank, a pip of a breeze on a covered porch, the reviving taste of sweet iced tea over a sweating glass of ice.

"Well, you found them. Now what are you going to do, or are you just going to stand here like a horse?" Bo spoke low so as not to disturb the scene before him. Whisky also stood motionless and quiet, ignoring Bo's comments, focusing instead on the fishing site.

"One thing is for sure: they don't know much about fishing. They're so loud they would spook Poseidon himself." Whisky rolled one of his ears back toward Bo and then slowly forward again.

"I recognize the colored kid, but I don't know the white one. The colored kid is the one we waved at awhile back. I see he has a friend now." He paused, chewed the inside of his cheek as he thought some more.

"Well, they're not doing any harm. I didn't have the heart to run off the colored boy back a few months ago. I can't see any reason to do it now, unless you have a problem with it." Whisky never changed his stance, just kept staring at the two boys as they enjoyed fishing and playing in the brilliant Texas sunshine. Bo soon found himself staring quietly too, captured at the simple joy in the moment, a quiver of a smile forming on his lips. He searched his memory banks, but came up penniless. He couldn't remember experiencing a similar happy time in his own youth.

"What a sad, old cowpoke I am," he said as he removed his cowboy hat and wiped his brow with an old handkerchief from his shirt pocket. He spent a few more minutes filling the void in his own memories with the spectacle before him.

"Whisky," he began talking to his horse with an exaggerated tone of authority, "if you're not going to walk over there and introduce yourself, then I think it's time we head to the barn."

Apparently now resolved that the situation held no danger and his duty was completed, Whisky swung his head around, signaling he was ready to go home. Bo held the reins ever so lightly between the fingers of his left hand and rubbed the old horse's neck with his right.

"Thanks, old man. I appreciate you leading me here. Sometimes folks don't recognize their own rough edges. Thank God for good horses who are part bloodhound."

When they returned to the barn, Clint was waiting and Matt was nowhere in sight. Bo dismounted next to the hitching post. Clint took the reins and looped them around the horizontal cedar post in preparation for Whisky's brushing.

"You let the boy go early?" Bo asked.

"Had to."

"Had to?"

"Yep, had to," Clint said. "All he did was complain about tending to the goats and waiting on you, so I sent him on. Can't stand a squalling child. Now I'm not complaining or anything of the sort, but I could use some more help around here. Maybe even some new help. Matt's more of a pain than he's worth. He ran off the last two young fellows your son sent out here from Houston. They said they quit because the drive was just too far, but the truth is Matt's aggravating enough to drive anyone away. They just didn't want to deal with Matt anymore."

"Is that the way you see it?"

"Yes sir, that's the way I see it, and that's the way it is." Clint's soft, gritty voice rose just slightly to emphasize his point.

"Well, I might have a replacement for those last two fellows sooner than you think. As for Matt, I sure would feel bad about letting him loose for somebody else to deal with. What do you say we give him a little more rope?"

"All you're doing is prolonging what you know is going to happen. The boy will use that extra rope to hang himself."

"I reckon I see your point. I'll study on it and let you know." Bo untied two leather straps from the back of his saddle in order to remove his saddlebags. He flung them over his shoulder and opened one of the flaps to remove a small, brown-paper lunch bag that held the second half of Whisky's apple. Bo stepped close to the horse, wrapped his arm under his head, and placed his hand palm up under Whiskys' muzzle to reveal the apple slice.

"Thank you, old bloodhound," he whispered into Whisky's ear, the horse flipping his upper lip to gently remove the apple from his rancher's hand.

My Dearest Mary Beth:

Today I caught two boys trespassing on the ranch. Usually I would have escorted them off the place with a warning that the law would be called the next time. Instead, I spent a great deal of time observing them at a distance behind Whisky's flickering ears. It gave me great comfort and pleasure seeing them play together. It made me feel sad and happy at the same time, missing the childhood I never had, but somehow being fulfilled through them. One boy was colored and the other white. I first saw them from pretty far away, as they ran without a care through the fields of tall grasses. Their fishing poles and gear did not slow them down a bit. I don't know why, but I didn't want to run them off the property like I would most times. I guess not having that kind of fun-filled childhood, I indulged myself in the simple thrill of it for the first time. Not even with our own kids have I had such a feeling. I was too busy being a provider, and the grandkids, I just don't see them enough. It made for an interesting, different kind of day.

# 21

"Well, you were right. There they are again," Bo whispered as he and Whisky emerged from the thick grove of trees on the back pasture side of Clear Creek. It was Saturday morning, another blazing day of beauty and leisure. Whisky had insisted on inspecting the back pasture again today, so Bo, sort of along for the ride, indulged him. They stopped for a moment at the end of the clearing.

Unaware of their audience, the boys sat quietly this time, concentrating on their fishing bobbers, which bounced up and down each time a fish nibbled.

"I think it's time we introduced ourselves."

Whisky stepped out into the clearing. As they approached, the boys turned and, without blinking an eye, innocently waved, as if their meeting was an everyday thing. Whisky stopped to inspect the lunch bag sitting on the ground behind the young fishermen. Bo was the first to speak.

"You boys having any luck?"

"Not yet. We just got here," Leonard replied, squinting his eyes upward, head pushed far back, so he could see Bo in the saddle.

The conversation stalled for a moment. Of his own volition, Whisky took a step forward to sniff up and down Leonard's neck, from his ear to the middle of his chest. The fine hairs and soft muzzle tickled Leonard. He broke into a fit of giggles, drawing his shoulders up tight to his neck, chin to his chest.

"Will he bite?" Kevin asked.

"Only apples," Bo replied, leaning forward over his crossed arms on the saddle horn.

"Can I pet him?" Leonard asked.

"He would be mighty disappointed if you didn't."

Both boys reached out and started to rub Whisky's muscular jawline and neck. They *oohed* and *aahed* in hushed tones.

"Is this his name?" Leonard pointed to the shiny brass plate riveted to the top of Whisky's bridle.

"Yes sir," Bo replied. "Gentlemen, meet Whisky by the Drink, Whisky for short."

"That's a funny name," Leonard said, wrinkling his nose.

"Not for a horse. You see horses are powerful animals so they need a name to match. Something with a little color . . ." Bo stopped himself. He was suddenly self-conscious about using the word "color" in front of this young boy. The boys hadn't noticed his stumble; they laughed and rubbed on Whisky, who happily returned the joy by wiggling his muzzle and nibbling their necks. Even though the boys had no reaction to the word color, Bo felt embarrassed and could feel his face start to flush. He quickly moved on.

"Kids, I'm Bo Kelso, the owner of this ranch. Where you boys from?"

Kevin and Leonard took turns, chatting happily about their homes, parents, school, and circumstances that drew them together. Bo sat atop Whisky, taking it all in. He admired the easy way the two of them flowed through their conversation, politely allowing the other to start and finish each other's sentences. They laughed a lot throughout their stories. Obviously, they were well-adjusted and happy boys. Through it all, they never stopped rubbing Whisky's neck. The horse showed his approval by holding still and closing his eyes as he dropped his head down so they did not have to reach up so high. Bo also approved, impressed by their candor and politeness.

Leonard then directed a question to Bo: "Mr. Kelso, is it okay for my friend and me to fish here? My mom told me to ask you, but I never did. I just figured it was probably okay since you never ran me off. But we probably should have asked." Kevin nodded in agreement.

"Well, there are some rules we need to cover," Bo said and leaned a little further over his saddle. The leather creaked and stretched as he eased forward to speak. "Don't mess with the livestock, especially the bull when he is in the front pasture. He will leave you alone if you stay clear of him."

The boys nodded their heads in unison.

"Stay out of all buildings and barns."

They nodded their heads even more emphatically. "We can do that."

They looked at each other, then Kevin asked, "If our parents ask, will you tell them that you gave us permission to play here?"

"I don't see why not."

"Well you see, we sort of told them that you gave us permission already. Because you saw me fishing here before, so . . ." Leonard's voice fell off.

"Oh, you mean back at the beginning of the school year, when I saw just you on the creek bank?" Bo sat up in the saddle and gathered Whisky's reins in his left hand.

Both boys nodded again.

"Well, I do recall tipping my hat, like this." He reached up with his right hand, lifted his hat, and dropped his head.

"Yes sir, I remember," Leonard replied.

"Well, when a Texan does that, it means the same thing as saying *It's okay*, or *How do you do*, or *Have a good day*. And to a lady, it's a sign of respect. A simple tip of a cowboy's hat can cover a lot of territory with one quick gesture. That's how we prefer to work."

Bo smiled as he saw a wave of relief in the boys' eyes, obviously happy to be lightened of the burden of their white lie. Besides, how could he say no to these young men and spoil what was surely a great adventure for them? "I do need you

boys to ask your parents something for me, if you're interested."
He paused for a moment, letting the moment linger. He noticed
with some satisfaction that the boys had frozen in anticipation
of his coming statement. Suddenly, he shook his head and said,
"Nahhhh. Never mind."

"What? What? What?" It was like a chorus of birdlike calls
as the boys insisted on details.

"Nah, I shouldn't have even brought it up. You boys are far
too puny to be ranch hands." Bo tried hard to keep his smirk at
bay, or worse, the burst of the laughter that was building in his
chest. He knew exactly what he was doing. He was dangling
the fresh bait, twitching the line to entice his prey to strike.

"Too puny? Ask our parents what?" Leonard spat out. "We
aren't too puny!"

"Ranch hands? Wait now, what do ranch hands do?" Kevin
questioned.

"Well," Bo started slowly, "ranch hands get paid money for
their hard work."

"We can work hard! Our size is deceiving. Leonard and I
unpacked my entire house in less than four days—just the two
of us."

"Hm," Bo hesitated just a bit more. "You'll have to be at work
at six o'clock in the morning. No kid likes getting up early."

"We do! We will!" Again the chorus.

"It's only for a few hours each day and you would still have
time off the rest of the day, and on weekends."

"But we have school during the week, sir," Leonard said.

"Well, I was thinking maybe after school is out, you can start
then. How 'bout that?"

Leonard and Kevin could barely squeak out a "yes" as they
nodded their heads so hard that Bo thought they'd fly right off
their shoulders. They looked at each other, their mouths round
as Cheerios.

"That sounds great, sir," Leonard said. Kevin just continued
nodding his head.

"Of course, we will have to clear it with your parents first.

I need to speak to them in person. I don't think I can just ride by the fence and tip my hat to them, if you get my drift." Bo winked his eye at each boy.

"Yes sir, we get your drift. Our parents will be home around four thirty today. Do you want us to have them call you? Today?" Kevin asked.

"Nope, livestock deals are always done face-to-face. I will come around tomorrow and make the deal in person. Now I need to make my rounds, so after you finish your fishin' trip, you two go up to the big barn yonder, on the other side of the main pasture." Bo turned in his saddle and pointed over his left shoulder. The barn was partially obscured by trees but easy to find. He continued, "Introduce yourselves to Clint. You can't miss him. He's a tall, wiry fellow, wobbles a bit when he walks. Clint runs the barn and takes care of the livestock. Tell him I sent you. He'll size you up for the job, so when you stand in front of him, ease up on your toes a bit so you look taller. Pull your shoulders back just a little bit, too, so you look bigger. And put a little bass in your voice, so you sound older."

He admired the way the boys were already practicing their stances. In their eyes he saw sheer excitement. It was as if Bo had given them free passes to the amusement park and money for all the rides. Then, as if some unspoken conversation had taken place between them, the boys gathered up their belongings as they thanked him repeatedly.

Bo held up his hands. "Whoa, whoa. You don't have to go right now."

"We know, but we can fish later," Kevin shouted over his shoulder as he broke into a sprint in order to catch up to Leonard, who already started running toward the creek.

"Whoa, where are you going? You're going the wrong way. You can use the bridge."

The boys stopped and turned toward each other.

"What bridge?"

"Well, how do you think I got here? There is a bridge that

crosses the creek just behind my house and the barn. Follow that trail yonder." He pointed along the ridge of the creek. "And it will take you straight to the bridge. You won't see it until you get right up on top of it. It will help keep your boots dry."

"Boots?" Leonard said, looking down at his muddy tennis shoes.

Kevin bolted toward the trail and passed Leonard.

"Hey, wait up!" Leonard yelled as he struggled to close the gap between them.

Bo sat for a minute in the silence and a dust cloud of youthful joy.

# 22

Bo returned to the barn around ten o'clock to find Clint waiting alone by the large, open barn doors next to his office. Bo tried to read his face as Clint held Whisky's bridle, tying him to the hitching post. As always, his face gave no hint at his thoughts.

"Did you have a nice ride?" As nonchalant as a spring breeze.

"Yep," Bo replied casually, angling for the same level of cool. He removed his saddlebags from Whisky's back and retrieved the apple slice from its brown paper wrap. He offered it to Whisky, who crunched it to a pulp with nary a drop allowed to fall. Bo threw the saddlebags over his shoulder, observing Clint as he loosened Whisky's saddle. No reaction. He couldn't stand it any longer. Clint was much better at these games than he was.

"Did the boys stop by and talk to you?"

"Yep," was his reply. Clint removed the saddle and walked to the tack room. Bo followed closely behind him, saddle blanket in hand.

"Well?" Bo persisted.

"Well what?"

"Do you think they will do a good job?"

"I hired them, if that's what you're getting at, and not just because you sent them up here. I must admit they are the puniest strays you ever brought home," Clint said.

"I was smaller than that when I started working stalls and wrangling cattle. I bet you were too."

"That's true. I bet those two never had to deal with someone like Matt though. He is already looking at the two of them sideways, 'specially the colored kid. I bet he is dreaming up all sorts of fun and games right now."

"Ah, it'll be okay," Bo said. "You and I dealt with bullies in the barn when we were kids, and we survived."

"That ain't true, Bo. You were the rancher's son. Whatever bullying you went through was tempered by the fact that your old man would fire someone for going too far, and I always had my brother close by. No one messed with the two of us. Plus we were tougher than a bag of hammers and packed the same kind of punch."

"That's true, but I think these two will surprise you. I see something in those boys. They can wrangle Matt just fine. If not, I am sure you will handle things."

Bo slapped Clint on the back for emphasis and started toward the house through the other end of the barn.

"You know those boys are in school until the second of June," Clint hollered after his boss and friend. "I can only work them in the mornings on weekends until then."

Bo paused by the chalkboard at the other end of the barn and turned toward Clint.

"Why, that should work out just fine. It will keep them clear of Matt for a while. That way, they can adjust. Now you don't have to worry so much."

"Yeah well, I just like it quiet around here on the weekends," Clint said.

"We all need to make a few adjustments to accommodate the new hands," Bo said, turning slowly to resume his walk to the house.

Clint popped his fist against the barn door, a smile on his face. "Well, don't that beat all."

He went back toward Whisky at the opposite end of the barn, grabbing a wide-bristle brush, twice the size of his palm, from atop a shelf by his office door. Whisky accepted the brushing with calm appreciation.

"How do you like that, old boy? Now we have to change our lives for two greenhorns."

Whisky leaned into the brush as Clint took long, sweeping strokes across his back and shoulders. Whisky curled his upper lip, showed his grass-stained teeth, and lightly shook his head.

"Yeah well, if that's what makes the boss happy, then that's what'll be done."

Clint moved to the other side of Whisky and started to brush again. Whisky stomped his right hoof on the ground and nodded his head—up and down, up and down. "You like that, don't you, boy?" He gave the horse one last long stroke and three firm slaps on the hip and said, "I've got to stop talking to the livestock. Somebody might hear and think I've lost my mind."

Whisky snorted and shook his head from side to side.

"Oh, not you. I don't mean you. I'm talking about the goats, old buddy."

Clint untied Whisky's reins from the hitching post and gently removed his bridle by lifting it over his ears and slipping it off his head.

"Now, sir, if you will join me in the dining room, I have prepared you an exquisite meal."

Clint walked toward Whisky's stall, and the horse followed closely behind without a lead. Dramatically, Clint held the stall door wide open with his right hand, bending slightly at the waist as he extended his left arm.

"After you, sir," he said as Whisky entered the stall. The bedding was fresh and clean, raked in long, perfect lines toward the door. Fresh cedar chips, one-inch thick, were spread throughout the ten-by-ten stall, emitting a pleasing aroma of clean earth and woods for man and equine alike.

Clint shook his head in admiration as he looked at Whisky,

royalty in this humble barn. Though he loved all the ranch horses and cared for them equally, Clint knew Whisky was the tie that bound the ranch and its people. And that was one tie that Clint didn't mind having.

# 23

"Dad, look! Here he comes," Kevin said to his father in an excited voice as he pointed in the direction of a Chevy truck bouncing through the middle of the pasture.

The pasture was smooth for the most part, though it did have the occasional anthill and cow pie. Watching out for cow pies in particular—he had no desire to waste time cleaning the unpleasant mess from the underbelly of his truck—Bo took his time negotiating his way through the lush, green, ankle-deep grass.

Just beyond the fence line, behind Kevin's house, a thin grove of hardwood trees spread their low branches, creating a perimeter about fifty yards wide, equally divided on both sides of the barbed wire fence. The grass on Kevin's side of the fence was a carpet of well-maintained St. Augustine, nestled in tightly to all the tree trunks. On the pasture side of the fence was a mixture of weeds and scattered, shade-loving grasses kept short by the grazing cattle and horses that perused the fence line at their leisure. The tree limbs swept low to the ground, but not so they blocked the view of the pasture dotted with wildflowers or prevented Bo from driving under and right up to the fence. Nor did they obstruct the pleasant breezes sweeping across the field through the grove.

It was early in the evening and several people from the subdivision had gathered at Kevin's house to enjoy Sunday dinner. The picturesque yard nestled in against the curving banks of Clear Creek provided a perfect backdrop for the meal.

Leonard's mom had been one of the first to arrive. Eight

more neighbors soon joined the swelling crowd. The smell of brisket, slow-barbecued and spiced to perfection, filled the air. The aroma gently rode the breeze that floated throughout the neighborhood. No need for a dinner bell to call the hungry fellowship.

Allen Ferris had set out three long tables, which were quickly filled with plates of food brought by everyone to enjoy. Mashed potatoes, sweet potatoes, red potatoes. Bowls of rice: brown, white, long grain, short grain, Spanish, and just plain sticky. Someone brought a propane heater to boil shrimp and blue crab big enough to pull a grown man off a boat. Kevin's mother made two large kettles filled with jambalaya and crawfish gumbo—so spicy that it might take two of the eight pitchers of sweet tea on the drink table to put out the fire in one's mouth.

As Bo approached, everyone's attention turned toward the sound of the truck. Whispers of gossip filtered through the crowd: "He's the richest man in Pearland; he might even be the richest man in Texas." Those who knew Bo personally showed their surprise that Bo was even driving up to a crowd of people—not the norm by a stretch over the past few years. One of Bo's oldest neighbors said to another in a low voice: "He's a bit reclusive since Mary Beth died. He doesn't get out much or associate with too many people. However, he is extremely generous. Each year, he donates a lot of money to several different churches and charities around the area."

A few neighbors at the Ferris gathering started walking to the fence in order to greet Bo. But no one could beat Kevin and Leonard to that job, having literally sprinted ahead of everyone else at first opportunity.

"Where's your horse, Mr. Kelso?" Leonard asked.

"It's Sunday; I gave him the day off," Bo said, stepping out of the truck to meet the boys at the fence.

As others approached, good-natured welcomes and hellos were exchanged amidst a flurry of handshakes. Kevin and Leonard moved aside as the adults engaged Bo in friendly conversation. Though a man of solitude, Bo was obviously a well-respected and well-liked man. Finally, Kevin's father made his way to the fence and introduced himself.

Bo smiled. "Glad to meet you, Mr. Ferris. I'm Bo Kelso. You are one of the people I came to see today."

"Please call me Allen. What can I do to help?"

Bo explained how he was there on official ranch business, wanting to speak to the boys' parents about a summer job for the boys.

Before Allen could respond, Jane had made her way over to the small crowd at the fence and interrupted with a fluster of her hands.

"Where are your manners, gentlemen? Why don't you invite this man to dinner and quit talking through the fence like it's visitation day at the prison?"

Everyone laughed, urging Bo to join them for food and more conversation. Kevin and Leonard immediately spread the barbed wire fence, placing their feet on the bottom wire and their hands on the next wire up to spread it. They looked up at Bo and waited.

"Nah. I can't stay for dinner. I've got to get back to the house," Bo said, but he lacked conviction.

"That's a shame, Bo," Allen said with a devilish grin. "My wife makes the best jambalaya this side of the Mississippi River. She makes it three ways: tasty, tasty and hot, and dangerously hot and tasty. And from all the food I've seen over there on the tables, we're going to have to invite an army to eat it all. You've got to help us!"

The boys spread the fence wider, so wide the nails started creaking at the point where it was hammered to the cedar fence posts. Their hands started to shake and quiver just a little, but they did not let the gap they had formed close even a fraction of an inch. They waited.

"Mr. Kelso, it would surely be a pleasure if you joined us all for Sunday dinner. Truth is, I'm not so famous for my jambalaya, but I am famous for my crawfish gumbo, and there's lots of it," Jane encouraged.

She was close enough to the fence where Bo could see her brilliant, deep-blue eyes. He realized there was no excuse for turning down such an offer from a beautiful woman and a friendly crowd. He had lied about needing to go home, and the kindness in her eyes assured him that she knew it, but was having none of it.

"Well, I am a little hungry, and honestly, I can barely stand my own cooking. Can you boys hold that fence just a little bit wider for a rickety old man?" he asked.

The boys strained and put as much muscle as they could muster into the task. Bo stepped across one leg at a time, passing through flawlessly, not snagging a single thread of clothing. By the time he'd cleared the fence and made his way over to the table, a place had been set for him and a large white dinner plate placed in his hands, so he could make his first pass at the table piled to the edges with food. He could have been the guest of honor for all the fuss. Everyone engaged him in conversation and showed their pleasure of his company.

With the addition of the one neighbor least expected to be present, the gathering was complete. Bo had often eaten dinner with his children and grandchildren before his wife died. Since her death, he had retreated into the farmhouse away from them, preferring to spend his time alone or in close proximity of the confines of the fence that surrounded the ranch. With his children so busy with their own lives, his isolation had become more a comfortable norm. It was a kind of personal exile that he did not realize affected him—until this very moment. He missed camaraderie such as this: the relaxation, the smells, the entangled conversations. There were bursts of joyous sounds as someone laughed aloud or the children squealed, running around and carrying on. Food was passed this way, that way, one plate trashed for a clean one, sweet tea splashing over cups of ice.

He briefly considered how far he had separated himself from others, and he understood why. It was the easiest thing to do. But that safety zone was false, an unhealthy cowardice, a complacency that even Bo loathed and knew would eventually let him down. But not today. Today was different, and today was better than yesterday. Was it possible this encounter had steered him from the dangers of a spiraling path downward?

After everyone had a plate or three of the good food, Bo spoke privately to the boys and Lynette, Jane, and Allen. All agreed that summer work at the barn would be a good thing for them. Allen joked, "If they're going to run amok on the property, they might as well be a part of its upkeep."

After getting the thumbs up, Bo looked at Kevin and Leonard to give them a final opportunity for escape and to offer them a challenge. "Now don't think it's going to be easy working on the ranch. It's nothing but hard work all the time. So if at some point it's too hard for you to wrangle it all, I will understand if you want to quit."

The boys looked at Bo, then their parents, then Bo again.

"We won't quit!" Leonard assured the group.

"We aren't quitters," Kevin offered, the final assurance everyone was looking for of the boys' commitment. A plan had been formed and commiserated upon. And summer was just a few weeks away.

Bo politely excused himself at this point, thanking everyone sincerely and enthusiastically, assuring Jane it was the most wonderful meal he'd had in years. Allen and Bo shook hands one last time.

"All right then," Bo said, "it's settled. You boys will work on the weekends until school is out, and then you will work on the days Clint needs you. Deal?" He engaged each boy's hand with a firm grip and a steady pump.

Their young hands were swallowed by Bo's large, calloused palm, but neither noticed. "Deal!"

After holding the fence wide for Bo to pass through, the boys watched as he climbed into his truck and drove away.

Bo looked in the rearview mirror, smiling to himself. He drove quietly and slowly toward the barn, leaving behind a firm foundation for friendships anew.

# 24

Both boys arrived at the barn right on time Saturday morning. Clint had met them just once, remembering only how puny they were. However, by the end of their first morning of work, he was genuinely impressed at their tenacity. They had strength and stamina he didn't remember having at that age. *Heck, they just might be an asset to the ranch after all.* Right away, the horses liked them, which was a good sign for Clint. They knew how to push a wheelbarrow, and were not afraid to fill it up to the very tiptop and push as hard as they could. Their backs would bow as the wheelbarrow plowed through the loose shavings piled up on the barn floor. They never spilled a single grain of feed or a drop of water as they hastily served breakfast to the twelve horses. Then it was on to the cattle, which were probably the easiest to feed; all the boys had to do was throw out four bales of hay and get out of the way.

The most fun they seemed to have was feeding the goats. The goats ran up on the boys as they carried their buckets inside the fence and surrounded them like seagulls fighting over chips. The goats nibbled at their clothes and jockeyed for position, attempting to shove their heads into the plastic five-gallon buckets of feed. The boys laughed hysterically—even Clint let out a chuckle—as they maneuvered their way through the hungry animals.

"Well, what do you think?" Bo asked Clint as he entered the barn, fresh cup of coffee in hand, just before the boys returned from the shaving box with clean bedding for the stalls.

"They're going to do a fine job. They catch on real quick and did everything exactly the way I told them to. They didn't even flinch when it came to cleaning out the stalls after I let the horses out. But that's just their first day, and they haven't met Matt yet," Clint said with a scowl on his face and a tone of remorse in his voice.

"I think they'll do just fine with Matt," Bo replied. He turned his cup upside down, emptying the last few drops on the thirsty ground at his feet.

"Yeah, we'll see how that works out," Clint said doubtfully.

———•———

The last remaining weeks of school passed quickly, and the temperature rose with each day, leveling out as it kept pace with a sweltering humidity. Kevin and Leonard showed up for work every weekend without fail. They never slowed down. In fact, they caught on so quickly to the routine of taking care of the animals that Clint was able to relax—a little.

And when the boys finally did run into Matt a time or two, Clint noticed they seemed to sense trouble and did their best to avoid him. Their instincts in this respect were admirable, and Clint was relieved.

Perhaps the biggest surprise of all was his boss, the unpredictably predictable Bo Kelso. Apparently, Kevin's mother had hand-delivered an invitation to Leonard and Kevin's junior-high graduation ceremony, which Bo had readily accepted. Leaving the house for the ceremony, he was a picture of cowboy fineness, dressed in a western-cut three-piece suit, black boots, and a matching Stetson. He was to sit with the boys' families in the audience and attend a small celebration at Leonard's house afterward. It was a day-long event that Bo had seemed quite excited to attend. No one was happier than Clint to see his boss venture out from the house, a change in character vastly different from the Bo of the last three years.

———•———

"Wow!" Leonard said as he stared in amazement at the large, oval belt buckle peeking from beneath Bo's tan dress jacket. It was partially hidden by his button-down vest. Bo lifted the vest up to expose the silver and gold buckle.

"That's the biggest 'n' shiniest belt buckle I've ever seen in my life," Leonard gasped.

Suddenly, everyone at Leonard's after-graduation party was staring at Bo's buckle. Bo made the most of it by sharing a little history.

"There are only two of these buckles in the whole world. Each was forged from the purest of silver. The roping rider on horseback here in the middle," Bo pointed with his finger, twisted the buckle a bit to reflect the overhead light, "it's made of twenty-four-karat gold. Me and a good friend of mine each won buckles at the Texas State Championship Rodeo in 1935. At the time, we were the best in the entire country at calf roping."

"It must be worth a lot of money," Leonard said, unable to peel his eyes away from the shining buckle.

"I reckon, but to me it is priceless. That means you can't put a value on it. It reminds me that I was once the best in the world at something, and that feeling can never be accented with a dollar sign."

As a graduation gift, Bo gave both boys two days' pay and the weekend off. They were to show up bright and early Monday morning for their first full week of work. He left the boys with a final warning about working on the ranch. "Horses don't know what day it is. They only know that they are hungry and that a man with a bucket and a cowboy hat can remedy that hunger. You have proven to me that you can do the work; now you have to prove to the animals that you will be there for them every morning, all summer long." Bo scanned their eyes slowly and deliberately, making sure once again that they understood the obligation of the job. But he knew in his heart that they wouldn't back down from their promise to him or to themselves. He admired their loyalty—to each other, to their new job—and the way they looked out for and relied on each other. They were a good combination for many reasons.

# 25

Leonard and Kevin finished their work at the barn just shy of ten o'clock. They were usually finished around nine, but Matt was extremely late that Monday morning, and the two of them had to work without him. When he did finally arrive around seven forty-five, most of the cleaning and feeding was completed except, of course, for the goats. Horses and cattle always came first.

"It is a good thing the goats are patient," Clint remarked as the boys hauled out the last bale of hay for the cattle that gathered in the fading shadows of the brightening dawn. Actually, Clint knew goats were patient only up to a point. They, too, had a way of letting everyone know it was their turn to be served breakfast. There were only six of them, but when they ran back and forth alongside the fence noisily sounding off in unison, one would think they were being slowly starved.

"I only have to spread out this last bale of hay for the cows, Mr. Clint, then I'll feed them and clean their bedding areas," Kevin said.

Clint looked directly at Matt, who was leaning lazily on one of the fence posts, drinking a Big Gulp, as he directed Kevin, "You just stay in the barn and finish up. Matt will take care of the goats."

"What? Why?" Matt blustered.

Disgusted, Clint did not acknowledge this reply and kept walking toward the barn door. A few minutes later, he told Kevin and Leonard they had performed a fine job and let them go for the day.

Bo hadn't made an appearance yet that morning, but Clint knew he was up and about—lights were on in the house. Even though the boys had a way of bringing out the extrovert in Bo, it was fleeting, and Clint had noticed a quiet distance settling in the old man lately, more so than usual. Maybe it was because it was getting close to the anniversary of Mary Beth's passing, which would lead to a series of other emotional events: their wedding anniversary a month later and her birthday the month after that. The summer months turned into a pile of wistful reminders for Bo. Clint felt more than a professional attachment to the ranch; he felt kinship and responsibility to the people here, especially Bo Kelso. As such, he guarded both man and beast with a quiet ferocity.

———•———

The full noonday sun reflected in wide, shimmering rays off the flat, steaming waters of the cattle tank. Dug into the top of the bluff, the tank sat just short of the large pecan grove on the edge of the main pasture where it wedged its way between the property line and Clear Creek. Kevin and Leonard sat quietly in the only spot of shade to be found along the banks of the one-acre tank. Close by Texas standards, it was still more than a mile from Leonard's back door and just as far from the barn. The dirt road that ran off the main paved road passed within twenty-five yards of the cattle tank and led to the main gate of entry for the ranch. It was a dehydrated mass of dust and gravel, dry as a preacher's throat after a three-hour sermon in a crowded clapboard church, with no fans on and the windows down.

The dirt cloud rose up from the road and hung in the air like fog, completely obscuring visibility for several minutes after a car had passed, or in this case a truck, Matt's truck.

The teen tore down the road, almost sliding sideways on the gentle curve that swung him to the right and onto the final stretch of road leading to the main gate. Matt obviously noticed the two of them sitting in the shade and fishing at the cattle tank because he started honking his horn and yelling at the top of his lungs, not in a friendly manner but in his normal taunting, condescending, bullying way. The dust floated over toward the boys and descended on them, causing them to choke and cough as they waved away the dust from their nostrils. "Jerk," they said in unison, only loud enough for the two of them to hear.

"I should've known he would do that," Leonard said as he struggled to spot his bobber floating in the tank.

"Yeah, me too. If it weren't so doggone hot, we'd be fishing on the creek, and he wouldn't be able to do that to us."

The heat was stifling—to the point where the boys kept their conversations short just to save them from breathing in the air that felt like it came out of the end of a torch. And to make things worse, now that scorching air was full of choking dust.

They turned their attention back to the water, but not for long. Kevin was the first to notice the sound of another vehicle coming down the road. They looked up, looked at each other, and Leonard groaned, "Here we go again."

It was Matt again; however, this time he was not on the road—he was in the pasture. Just short of the boys, Matt turned his truck hard to the left and gunned the motor. The boys could see his hands slapping one over the other on top of the steering wheel as the grill of his truck emerged from the lingering dust. The back end of the truck swung around hard and fast as the tires broke traction and spun, throwing gravel and dirt over the boys. The spray also peppered the ground around them and spread across the top of the water like raindrops. The boys quickly stood and covered their faces with their hands and started backing into the tree line, dropping their fishing poles.

Just a few feet from the boys, Matt stopped his truck after coming full circle, a neat doughnut. He revved his motor one time for effect. Dangling his left arm out the window, he flung his head back as he pounded his right hand on top of the steering wheel. He laughed like a jackal, snorting in between breaths and flinging his head forward and back.

The boys stayed quiet, unmoving, in hopes that Matt would become bored with his childish pranks and go away. They sensed this was a small taste of Matt's capability for cruelty. As long as he stayed in his truck, he could laugh all day long. Their discomfort seemed to entertain Matt greatly, which was fine. They were just thankful for the safety of the pecan grove, to which they had rapidly retreated in self-defense.

The dust had almost completely cleared by the time Matt finished laughing.

"Man, you should've seen the look on your faces. Hey, did you pee your pants?"

The thought of soiled britches apparently struck Matt as very funny, and he started laughing hysterically again.

And still, the boys did not move. Even the two of them together were no match for the likes of Matt.

"Hey, lighten up you two. Can't you take a joke?"

Of course, this was not a joke to the boys. It was disturbing harassment, a bigger person scaring a smaller one just for the morbid rush of it.

In a quick movement, Matt leaned forward in his seat. Both Leonard and Kevin drew a rapid breath, thinking Matt was reaching for a gun or something equally dangerous. They would not put it past him to produce a weapon and begin his next game.

Matt's head reappeared in the window. He had the cigarette lighter in hand, pulled a Winston from behind his ear, and lit it.

"You fellows want one?" he asked with a smirk.

"We don't smoke," Leonard blurted out.

Kevin heard a hint of arrogance in Leonard's voice and hoped Matt did not detect it. Bullies did not need much of a reason to be pushed over the edge and turn a simple taunting into a full-out physical assault. *The less we say, the sooner he'll go away.* At least he hoped so.

Playing possum was not easy for Kevin and Leonard. They were accustomed to taking a stand, sticking up for themselves.

They'd encountered bullies before, but they were usually of the same age, maybe a little stronger, but comparable. The boys knew that if it came down to a fight, they would fight, and give and take their licks. However, Matt was, in their eyes, an adult. He did not fit the profile of a schoolyard punk. Matt was out of school, had a full-time job, a part-time job, lived on his own; he even had a driver's license, could go and do as he pleased, and had to answer only to himself. Kevin and Leonard were baffled as to why he even wasted his time tormenting them.

Matt took a long drag on his cigarette, leaned his head back on the truck seat, and exhaled smoke out the window. The air was so still; the tendrils hung above the roof of his truck, slowly spreading across it, fading into long sheets as it disappeared into the air and the bed of his truck.

"So when do you girls go back to grade school?" Matt asked.

"We're in junior high, not grade school!" Leonard snapped back, this time with an unmistakably sharper tone in his voice.

Kevin nudged his friend with his elbow; Leonard was getting dangerously close to poking the bear. The look on Matt's face changed. His brow wrinkled as his eyes narrowed, and his lips tightened. There was no mistaking the look—it was as clear as the warning of a rattlesnake. Matt would control the tempo of his torment, not the poor mouse he was toying with.

With menace in his eyes, Matt said, "Well, I'll let you girls get back to playing with your fishing poles. You do know that the cows crap and pee in that tank, don't you? You may as well eat a turd out of the sewer, 'cause that's what those fish are swimming in."

With that, he turned his truck around and began to drive away. Backs turned, the boys braced themselves for another pummeling of grass and gravel. Instead, they were surprised to hear only Matt's bitter cackle as he slowly drove away. When the boys determined the truck was far enough away to keep them safe from another spraying of earth, they turned in his direction, staring at the back end of the old pickup as it tooled down the road.

Kevin gave Leonard a half punch in his upper arm. "Ouch, what was that for?"

"You need to keep your mouth shut around that guy."

"Why? I'm not afraid of him."

Kevin searched Leonard's eyes and saw that was just the tough guy in him talking.

"Let's go fishing somewhere else." Leonard started gathering up his fishing gear.

"Are you afraid of what he said about the fish swimming in the cattle's toilet?"

"No." Leonard paused a beat. "I'm afraid he'll come back and run over us next time."

Kevin let out a quick laugh, reached up, and put his hand on Leonard's shoulder as they turned and walked toward the edge of the cattle tank.

Just as they reached for their fishing poles, they saw movement on the other side of the pecan grove.

"Oh . . . that's why he didn't blast us with dirt," Kevin gave a quick nod of his head.

"What do you mean?" Leonard said, turning around.

"He saw Mr. Kelso coming. That's why."

Bo was making his final swing around the backside of the main pasture, easily seen through the pecan grove.

The boys' arms were flying above their heads in greeting. Bo acknowledged their enthusiastic wave with a tip of his hat. He asked if the boys were having any luck fishing. Confessing their lack of success, they told him they were just considering moving to another fishing hole.

"It's hot enough to fry a frog on his third hop across an asphalt driveway. It's definitely not the right kind of weather for sitting out in the sunshine baking your brains under your hat while you wait on the fish that's as cool as he can be. Don't you think so?" Bo asked.

"Yes sir, but if we go home, there is nothing to do except maybe whatever my mom comes up with—probably girly stuff around the house," Leonard said earnestly.

Bo chuckled at this. "Girly stuff, huh? What does that include exactly?"

"You know . . . sweeping, gathering laundry, dusting, all sorts of stuff. My mom looks after this girl Jenny, and she's into all that girly stuff too."

Leonard's mother watched over the boys and one other girl during the summer. Jenny was seven years old and lived on their road. The epitome of a girly-girl, she always wore summer dresses and shoes to match, her blond hair short with flowing curls. She and Leonard's mom were always baking something—and not just simple things like cookies. Any variety of elaborate cakes and pies could adorn the kitchen table at the end of the day, decorated to perfection, every one. Jenny would threaten the boys with a wooden spoon any time they passed through the kitchen, warning them to keep their hands off. Short for her age, her head barely cleared the kitchen counter. What she lacked in height, she made up for in tenacity.

Leonard's mother and Jenny would spend at least two hours a day reading to each other. It was a package deal for Jenny's parents. Leonard's mom watched Jenny, tutored her, and indulged her.

"Jenny is seven going on twenty-five. And bossy," Leonard complained.

"I see," Bo said. "Still it's awfully hot to be fishing out here at the edge of an open pasture. Why aren't you fishing in the old sand mine on the back of the property? The water is crystal clear, and most of the bank is shaded down two sides. The water is only knee deep on a tall coon dog off the bank and as clear as a glass of spring water. You boys can swim there, as long as you stay close to the shore and stay together."

Each began to bounce on his toes. "I am an excellent swimmer, Mr. Kelso. I was on the swim team at my old school," Kevin said.

"And I took swimming lessons at Johnson's pool up the street last year—in the advanced class," Leonard said.

"You don't have to worry about us," Kevin added with conviction.

"Where is it at, Mr. Kelso?" Leonard asked.

"I thought you knew. I have seen the two of you all over this ranch each time I rode the fence line, trotting across the fields and thickets like two armadillos tied together by rope."

Eyes wide with the idea of it, the boys quickly looked at each other. They didn't remember seeing the old rancher that frequently.

"Oh yes, I saw the two of you many times, long before we met and said our hellos, running fast, laughing loud, while Whisky and I walked slow and talked low. Yep, you sure were easy to find on Saturdays and sometimes during the week after school."

As he spoke, he dismounted Whisky and walked the horse over to the water's edge, allowing him to drink. He stood beside him and worked his hands slowly and smoothly, one behind the other, across the horse's hips and over his tail until he reached the other side of Whisky's saddle. He never broke contact with his horse's body, reassuring his horse in doing so. Then Bo raised his arm and drew the boys' attention in the direction of the tallest pine trees on the other side of Clear Creek.

"Beyond those tall, yellow pines is a grown-over dirt road. The saplings popped up like corn and choked off the road down to a small trail just wide enough for a man on horseback, or maybe . . . two excited boys running side by side. Following that trail until it runs out at the sand mine should get you to a small beach. I ride Whisky there at least once a week and let him walk out into the water to drink and cool down. From the saddle, I can see hundreds of fish darting around in that water. No one has fished there in years. It's been hidden by the overgrowth because there are no longer enough cattle to eat away at the plants and keep them set back. I was sure you boys would've found it by now."

The boys stared with great interest, hanging on every word

that their old friend spoke. If their eyes could have gotten bigger, they would have needed more room on their heads. With each syllable of description, they leaned in a little closer. This story about the sand mine was, to them, like describing the location of a lost treasure buried in a far-away, mysterious country. They were so excited about this secret that they did not even care about the fact that the beach was more than three miles away. In the blistering heat. One way.

"Can we fish there?" Kevin excitedly asked.

"I don't see why not. You two have fished everywhere else." Bo tried for deadpan, but a grin was peeping through his façade. The boys hastily grabbed their fishing rods and tackle, running at a full sprint toward the bridge—the fastest route to the creek—shouting "Thank you, Mr. Kelso" to the beat of their pounding steps.

In a rare fit of mischief, Bo mounted Whisky and laid out the reins. He gave him a gentle kick with his heels, and the horse launched forward, almost rearing up off his front hooves. Off to the races.

Within a few seconds, he'd passed the two running boys. Whisky flipped his tail wildly, head held high as he stretched out into a full gallop. Bo knew the horse was in his element, enjoying the rare treat of running with abandon. Whisky snorted loudly as he passed the boys, as if to say, "Tag! You're it. Catch me if you can."

Bo reached the barn well ahead of the boys and pulled back slightly on the reins. Whisky responded by slowly decelerating to a trot.

———•———

The sound of Whisky's hooves pounding on the ground caught Clint's attention. He'd been taking a short nap propped up in his chair just inside his office door. He reluctantly cracked open one eye and then the other. He was comfortably settled into his desk chair, both legs kicked up on top of the small wooden crate jammed between the filing cabinet and the far wall. The springs of the old wooden office chair creaked as they uncoiled when Clint leaned forward.

"Now what can that be all about?" he whispered in a low growl.

He knew Bo would not return for at least three hours, and this was one of the best fifteen minutes of the day for him usually, just a fraction of time that he and the cats cherished together—everyone gone, chores completed, radio playing softly. The only thing left to do for Clint was to brush down Whisky after his morning ride.

Although it was hot outside, a slight breeze blew through the barn, and a small fan with four metal blades cooled his face and kept the flies away. Even the two barn cats curled up in their favorite spots, one on the far corner of the wide windowsill just above the filing cabinet and the other on the box full of magazines just outside the office door. This ruckus was definitely an intrusion on their happy place.

# 26

Clint sat straight up in his chair and placed his feet on the floor. Reluctant to rise, he peered out his door and could see Bo tying Whisky to the hitching post.

"Back so soon?"

"Yep; change of plans."

"Just leave Whisky. I'll get to him. Is everything okay?"

"Yep."

"You sure?"

"Yep."

Clint recognized a tone of heightened excitement in Bo's voice. Curious, Clint walked to the edge of the barn door, where he saw Kevin and Leonard closing in fast, their fishing poles swinging wildly back and forth as they ran.

"You sure everything is all right?"

"Yep, why do you keep asking me that?"

"That's the first time I've seen you run Whisky in years, and you got those two youngsters choking back your trail dust. Everyone's in a hurry, except the cats and me. So I guess maybe I should be asking 'What's going on?' instead of 'Are you all right'?"

"Oh I'm fine, just fine. I'm going fishing."

Bo was more charged up than Clint had seen him in years. There was a time years ago, before his wife had become ill, when his smiles and laughter were more common. He was happiest when the whole family—Mary Beth, kids, grandkids—would ride the pastures together. All the saddles and tack were utilized to outfit every horse in stock for those day-long trail rides. Sometimes, especially in the fall, more than twenty riders would leave out from the ranch and ride into Pearland some twelve miles away for a rodeo or fair. They would return before dark, worn out and tired. The grandchildren, some of them only four or five years old, rode double, hanging onto their parents' backs, sound asleep. Bo and Mary Beth would trail their riderless horses behind. Just looking at Mary Beth and Bo during those times, anyone could see the signs of pure and unconditional love.

And here Clint was seeing that excitement again in his old boss, in a new way.

"Fishing!" he hollered out in disbelief. "You don't fish."

Without offering a reply, Bo stretched out his steps and rushed out the other end of the barn to get in his truck. He started it and drove around the barn to the end of the bridge where he intercepted the two boys just before they started to cross. Clint was awestruck. He'd not seen Bo do anything that wasn't a planned event. And this little excursion was most certainly anything but planned. It was . . . spontaneous. A word rarely used to describe Bo Kelso.

Clint watched as the boys jumped into the back of the pickup truck, first tossing in their poles and gear and then, with the agility of youth, their bodies. Their leap from the ground to the bed of the truck was as if they'd popped off a trampoline, barely touching the sides. Once they settled in, Bo took off, almost spinning the tires.

Still standing next to Whisky, Clint removed his hat and scratched his scalp, perplexed and happy at the same time. Not sure exactly what had just happened, he turned to Whisky.

"Do you know what's going on?"

Whisky jerked up his head slightly and shook his bridle.

"Well, whatever it is, I like it."

Whisky snorted in agreement, turning his head in the direction of the bridge.

# 27

Bo stopped his blue Chevy short-bed just before the overgrown road that led to the sand mine. The trail had once been the main thoroughfare for dump trucks that ran in and out with loads of sand, an extremely valuable resource necessary for the foundations of buildings and roads. Bo and the boys started walking down the cluttered path together.

"I'm sure glad you came with us, Mr. Kelso. I don't think we would have found it without you," Leonard politely said.

"Oh, I'm sure you would have, but you'd be tuckered out by the time you did."

"That's for sure," Kevin replied, wiping spider webs from his face.

The invisible strands stretched across the path about head-high and were numerous, but not to the point that they dampened the spirits of the adventurers, young and old. Bo had made this trip hundreds of times, especially when he'd been able to drive through here in the early '60s to check on the operation. The sand mine was one of Clay's first business ventures.

The trail started to widen as they got closer to the water.

"This way?" Kevin asked as he pointed and looked over his shoulder at Bo, who was bringing up the rear.

"Yep, right through there."

The saplings were thick and no more than three or four inches apart. The limbs hung low and were full with leaves. Pine, gum, mimosa, yaupon, and magnolias, all of them full, crowded together in a choking blockade. All manner of vines grew up and into the fifteen-foot tall trees, joining them together like an awning blocking out the sun before it could touch the ground.

"Oh my God!" Kevin screamed dramatically as he reached the edge of the mine.

Then Leonard: "Oh my God, this is incredible."

The boys reacted as if they had never seen water before. They waded into the water holding their rods and small tackle boxes. The water was as cool as ice water because of the long shadows cast upon it from the thick overgrowth and tall pines that firmly held together the bank. They were awestruck at their surroundings and stood motionless, soaking in the magnificence of this hidden paradise. Bo's description of the clarity of the water was not even close to the reality of it. The greens were greener than anything they had ever seen. The shallow water was translucent and deceptively deep. Out toward the corner of the mine, the water reflected the spectacular white clouds against the intoxicatingly blue sky. The water was so flat that they could see the heavens above them in perfect, unbroken reflections without looking up.

Bo stopped at the edge of the clearing and was again reminded of the true beauty of this haven, brought to life by the words and expressions of two young boys, bound together by an inseparable friendship. He watched them just standing in the water, scanning the banks, stretching their gazes across the spectacle surrounding them.

Bo sat down on a fallen, dead pine tree, its diameter so large that he perched comfortably atop it. He missed this, what he had not had as a young man—just being a boy. He had always been a rancher, a provider, and the responsible one. Mary Beth was his joy and his children and grandchildren his life, and a good life it had been; but he never got to do what these two boys now so effortlessly did. Their only responsibilities were to be good sons, love their parents, and show up for dinner on time, do a chore, do homework. Soon they would become young men and life would accelerate, and Bo was sure they would keep pace with it. But for now, they were boys. He knew in the years and decades to come, Kevin and Leonard would fondly reflect back on this part of their lives as clear in reflection as the water in which they now stood. Through them, Bo filled part of his soul with this missing piece of his past.

His trance was broken when Leonard yelled out, "Holy cow! Look at the size of that bass! There's another one, and another one. Hurry, get the bait out. Oh my God, they are everywhere. There's more over there." They were both yelling now.

The abandoned sand mine was alive with fish and beauty. The boys frantically ran back to the shore and rigged their baits so they could cast into the massive schools of bass, yellow perch, and crappie. The fish fearlessly swam close to them and exposed themselves. The smaller ones nibbled at the boy's legs. They cast out in front of them several feet, and each time, their bobbers were immediately jerked under and disappeared from sight. They retrieved their catches, re-baited their hooks, and recast. Each cast yielded a fish, which seemed to be getting bigger and bigger each time.

Bo sat quietly watching them, completely engrossed in their joy.

Leonard screeched with excitement after landing a particularly large fish. "Look at the size of this one, Mr. Kelso!"

Bo just nodded his head and waved his hand. He did not want to interrupt this experience, not for the boys and not for himself. He knew this was a benchmark in their lives, even though they didn't know it yet. More importantly, Bo was taken with what he had missed as a boy in having a best friend. Only with a trusted buddy could such joy come from exploring and fishing and goofing around. He was happy to share in this tiny slice of life that had long since passed for him.

"I got another big one, Kevin," Leonard yelled. "Mr. Kelso, here." Leonard backed his way out of the knee-deep water, reeling and fighting a largemouth bass. The Zebco reel sounded like a bicycle chain attempting to change gears. The drag reluctantly relinquished the monofilament line to the frantic fish as it darted hard left then right. The rod bent, doubled over from the strain of the scaly monster. Leonard continued to back his way out of the water and onto the short, sandy bank.

"Here, Mr. Kelso. Take it. Take it!"

"No, you're doing a fine job, boy. You keep at him," Bo encouraged, laughing.  He refused to deprive Leonard of this mighty fight.

Bo kept waving Leonard back, but it was no use. Finally able to reach him, Leonard thrust the rod and reel into Bo's hands. The old man was astonished at the feel of the line, as it pulled and jerked wildly. He widened his eyes and tightened his grip.

"Uh-oh. That's some kind of pull. Here, Leonard, you pull him in," he said and tried to pass the rod back to Leonard.

Leonard held up his hands and backed away. Truth was, Bo didn't really want to give the rod back to Leonard, but he didn't know how to work the reel. He'd never been fishing before and refused to admit he didn't know what to do. So, he stood there, holding the rod, marveling at the sensation as the fish continued to peel off line.

Meanwhile, Kevin had hooked another bass. "I got another one!"

In order to keep his fishing line from tangling with Bo's, Kevin backed out of the water and stood beside him. Bo's hands were gripped so tightly below the reel—in the wrong spot—that his knuckles were white from the pressure. Bo looked down at Kevin with a shrug of his shoulders and a weak smile, and Kevin concluded that this big rancher man had no idea what to do with a fishing pole. He started a quick lesson.

"Hold it like me. That's right; now turn that handle and get back some line, or you'll get ripped off."

"Ripped off?" Bo couldn't contain the excitement in his voice.

"Yeah, the drag will pay out all the line until it breaks. So crank the handle and pump the rod until you get your line back."

"Okay! Got it!"

Bo was exhilarated. He followed Kevin's instructions, but the bass, a mighty fighter, took back all of Bo's gains on the next furious run. "He just pulled all my line off again. Is there some way of stopping him from doing that?"

Both boys started laughing aloud, so hard they honked.

Leonard regained composure first. "You got to just keep cranking it back each time he takes it away, Mr. Kelso. That's fishing. That's the fun."

Bo acknowledged Leonard's advice by nodding his head vigorously in agreement, his smile wide and hearty.

"Wow! I just got a look at his tail," Leonard cried out as he jumped up and down, running back and forth on the sandy shoreline. He looked like a teammate running on the sidelines as one of his friends ran the football down the open field to the goal line for an unobstructed touchdown. And his elation was contagious. Now all three were yelling in unison as the monster bass shot into the air and jerked his head violently several times before crashing back into the sparkling water.

Bo turned to Kevin and yelled, "Did you see that?" His voice was not his own, his pitch noticeably higher and profoundly happy. "That's the biggest fish I've ever seen in my life!"

Leonard was still on the shore, running and jumping. Kevin finally managed to subdue his fish and add it to the growing stringer. Laughter was everywhere at the same time, like bubbles blown into the air, floating aimlessly, playfully.

Suddenly, Bo felt something pull up inside of him, something powerful and serene. He didn't quite understand what was happening, but the calm moved through his body, and for a moment, all was quiet and still. He was completely focused on the intensity of this peace. He was jubilant.

He turned his gaze to the heavens and noticed a slight breeze move the treetops then slide down onto the calm waters of the sand mine. The monofilament line sliced the glasslike water as the behemoth bass ripped to the left and right. Everything else was still. It was so quiet that Bo swore he could hear the fine fishing line whistling through the water, placid in its posture.

Then, a cool breeze came from the heavens. It raced across the water, straight at him, causing the calm water to bristle. That is when he heard it: his wife's voice, tender, comforting, and low.

*"Bo, my love."*

*Splash!* The giant sprang into the air once more, tail dancing across the water in a last ditch effort to spit the hook. The atmosphere returned to normal, sounds and sensations in full swing, the boys again yelling in delight, and the reel screaming and struggling against the bass, though not as loud and not as much. The fish was giving in to the newfound talents of this fledgling angler.

The battle was won, and now Leonard and Kevin waded out into the water to stand beside Bo as he took his last few cranks of the reel and brought it alongside his legs. Bo looked down. It wasn't until that very moment that he realized he'd been standing knee-deep in the water, cowboy boots filled, Levis soaked a dark blue up to the hips.

Kevin reached out and landed the worn-out fish by pinching his thumb and forefinger around its bottom lip. "Holy jumpin' horny toads, Mr. Kelso, he's got to be ten pounds."

Kevin firmly placed his other hand under the tail of the beaten bass and held them up parallel to the water. Silence had returned, mouths agape, as they marveled at the mighty, regal fish. Leonard pinched the hook and gave a slight twist; it fell from the fish's mouth with barely any effort.

"He was barely hooked, Mr. Kelso," Leonard said, incredulous.

Kevin held up the fish. "Here you go," he said, offering the fish to Bo.

Bo handed the rod and reel to Leonard and eagerly reached

out for his landed prize. "Oh my, I think you're right. He is about ten pounds."

"Is that the biggest fish you ever caught?" Kevin asked, smile beaming.

"That's the first fish I ever caught in my life, boy, and thanks to the two of you, my first *and* biggest."

Bo looked again at his beautiful catch. He stared at it, as if it was a solid gold brick he tripped over while walking in the grass. Kevin and Leonard gave each other a look of disbelief.

"Your first, really?" Leonard asked.

"Yep, my very first."

Leaning forward, Bo gently lowered the fish, belly first, into the water. Its tail made a gentle swishing action back and forth. Opening both his hands, spreading his fingers wide and his palms up, the fish slowly slid out of his hands and turned toward the boys. Its dorsal fins and tail barely moved as he swam between them, standing no more than two feet apart. Two more short swings of his tail and the fish had passed the boys. They turned to watch the departure.

It was a great show, almost as if Bo and the great fish were in cahoots: *I'll let you catch me, if you promise to let me go.*

A bubble rose from the fish's mouth, wiggled up to the surface, and popped like a giggle just an arm's length away. Then the fish disappeared from sight.

The boys could not believe that Bo had released the fish. They turned to look at their new fishing friend, who looked so content and natural, hip high in the still water.

"Well, who's going to catch him next?" Bo said, though he had difficulty getting the words from his mouth, as if he'd just woken up from a deep slumber. Both the boys began to frantically cast in the direction of the fish.

Bo returned to the log and removed his boots and socks, emptying the water from his Lamas and ringing out his socks. He then bent over, rolled his pant legs two or three times up to his calves, and wiped a joyful tear from his cheek.

# 28

"Where is your nigger friend?" Matt taunted as he entered the barn from the back side, late as usual.

Kevin could smell beer on Matt's breath and figured he'd been out most of the night with his friends partying, up to no good. Matt was obviously referring to Leonard, who was late himself. Arriving on time, he'd started cleaning stalls by himself while Clint fed the horses at the other end of the barn. Kevin ignored Matt's question as he continued to scoop manure from the bottom of the stall and drop it into a wheelbarrow. Matt leaned further into the stall, both his arms crossed just under his chin on the stall wall.

"Hey, greenhorn!" Matt said as he kicked his boot on the bottom board of the stall in order to get Kevin's attention.

Kevin had heard him the first time but didn't want to answer. He knew Matt had a mean streak and was always looking to bully someone. With Matt being much stronger, older, and bigger, he felt the best strategy was to avoid confrontation. If he said the wrong thing, Matt would surely make his life miserable in every possible way.

"I said, where is your nigger friend? Have you gone deaf?"

———————

Leonard was about to enter the open barn door no more than ten feet behind Matt. However, when he heard Matt refer to him as a "nigger," he stood frozen in his tracks. *What now?* His heart and head pounded with confusion and indecision.

Aware of the nasty disposition of his fellow ranch hand,

Leonard weighed his options. On the bully scale of one to ten, Matt was a perfect ten.

Careful not to make a sound, Leonard slowly took a step backward into the shadow of the barn door, just out of sight. He could not see them, but it was easy enough to hear the conversation, even though Matt's volume was fairly low. Probably so Clint couldn't hear him.

"I'm not deaf," Kevin replied.

"Well, we've established you ain't deaf. Now where is your nigger friend?"

"He's just running a little late. He should be here in just a few minutes."

"Why do you hang around with him anyway? Can't you find any white friends? Hell, you'd be better off hanging around a Mexican than a black boy."

Silence.

"You know, I don't have much tolerance for tardy black boys. I might have to fire that boy."

Leonard knew that Matt didn't have the authority to do that; he was just flexing his muscle and being what he was, a bully. Still, he waited.

"So, I guess you hang around Leonard because you don't know how to find any white friends, is that right?"

Silence.

"You know what that makes you? That makes you a nigger lover, and there ain't nothing lower on the face of this earth than that. That makes you worse than your friend."

Matt sounded like he was becoming more and more agitated because Kevin wasn't responding to his barbs. *Why wasn't he responding to his barbs?*

From further down the barn, Leonard heard Clint: "Matt! Get down here and start on the eastside stalls before I send you home."

"Yes sir, Mr. Clint. I'm on the way right now," Matt hollered back, then in a softer tone, "I guess I will talk to you later, nigger lover."

The conversation now over, Leonard still had a choice to make. Enter the barn? Discuss what he'd heard? Go home?

Chewing on the side of his thumbnail, he made up his mind. He turned and walked back across the pasture to his house.

The sun had not quite stirred up enough light for his silhouette to be obvious. He moved quickly and quietly, a horrible pain in his chest. Betrayal, that's what he was feeling. He felt betrayed by Kevin. Even though Matt was much bigger and stronger, Kevin could have said something, put up some sort of resistance to that hateful speech. Leonard's emotions were many: anger, remorse sadness, fear. And loneliness, like he hadn't a friend in the world who would stand up for him. At the same time, he was thankful he had not walked in that barn and been made to endure the verbal and possibly physical brutality that Matt could surely dish out.

---

The morning passed slowly as stalls were cleaned and horses fed and items on the chalkboard checked off. Bo emerged from the ranch house and greeted everyone as he walked to Whisky's stall. Without much conversation other than the standard greetings, he saddled up and rode off toward the back portion of the pasture, the same as he did most mornings.

Clint's eyes followed them for a few minutes. He inhaled deeply the smells of a ranch morning, thinking about Kevin and Matt and what was going on between them. He could sense the tension and managed to keep them separated, performing tasks at opposite ends of the barn and outside buildings. At nine o'clock, Clint gave the okay for Kevin to knock off for the day. He held back Matt, on the other hand, to perform a few more tasks, but mostly to keep him from harassing Kevin on his way home.

Kevin strode quickly through the property, heading straight in the direction of Leonard's house. His buddy had never missed work before.

Kevin fretted, each step adding a new worry to his mind: Did he oversleep? Is he sick? Did something happen at home? Is someone hurt? Multiple scenarios reeled through his mind, all leading to one conclusion. Worried for his friend, Kevin needed to get to him as quickly as possible. He picked up the pace.

The walk across the pasture was about five hundred yards to Leonard's back door. It only took him a few minutes to reach it, but the time seemed much longer to him. He knocked. Leonard's mother opened the door wide, greeting him with a friendly smile.

"Well, good morning, Kevin. How are you?"

"Fine, Mrs. Parker. Uh, is Leonard okay?"

"Why do you ask that?" Lynette's face dropped to a frown.

"Because he didn't show up for work this morning."

"Are you sure? I heard him get up this morning and leave."

Concerned, she turned and headed in the direction of Leonard's room, which was at the very end of the long hallway. Kevin followed close behind her. They passed the kitchen where Leonard's cereal bowl was still sitting on the table. Now more horrible thoughts were creeping into Kevin's head. *What if something happened to Leonard on the way to the ranch? What if he was injured walking in the dark across the pasture? What if Matt got to him?*

Kevin wouldn't put it past Matt to ambush Leonard and beat him up, leaving him out in the grass, lying in a pool of his own blood, unable to call for help, wondering who would come looking for him and when. Yeah, that had to be it. Matt had hurt Leonard! Before Matt got to the barn, he'd ambushed Leonard and then acted as if nothing was wrong. *My God, I may have walked right past him lying in the grass. I've got to go back and save him.*

As he thought through all of this, Mrs. Parker approached Leonard's room and knocked on the closed door. Kevin's train of thought came to a stop when Leonard's muffled voice responded.

"Leonard, are you okay? Kevin is here to see you." Lynette opened the door to find her son face down on the bed. "Leonard?"

"Go away, Kevin. I don't want to talk to you."

Shocked, Lynette said, "Leonard! What in the world—?"

Kevin interrupted. "It's okay, Mrs. Parker." He was just as confused as she was, but he didn't want to make it any worse.

Leonard's mother nodded her head and pursed her lips. "I'll just leave you boys to talk then," she said. She gently ushered Kevin into the room and closed the door behind her, leaving the boys to work out things between themselves.

"Kevin, I don't want to talk to you." Leonard was emphatic in his tone, but his voice quivered slightly.

*Is he angry?* Kevin said, "Come on, Leonard, what's wrong? I've been worried, thinking you were sick or hurt or something. Why didn't you come to work today?"

No reply.

"Why won't you talk to me?"

No reply.

Panic began to take hold. "Okay, are we still going fishing?"

"No!"

"Why not?" Kevin suddenly wanted to cry he was so frustrated. He wanted to know what the problem was so he could understand Leonard's mood. But it didn't look like Leonard was going to help him out on this one. He tried again, "Okay, enough of this. Come on and tell me what's wrong with you, Leonard."

Leonard rolled over and yanked the pillow off his head. He threw it down on the bed.

"You!" he spat. "You're what's wrong. I heard every word Matt said, and I heard every word you DIDN'T say!"

Kevin threw his hands up in the air, his face a ball of tension. "What are you talking about?"

"I *did* make it into work this morning. I was standing outside the barn door and heard your conversation with your *buddy* Matt."

"I didn't see you there. Why are you saying this?" Kevin's tone was defiant, but his mind was transitioning to a slow realization.

"That's because you were too busy . . . with your new friend. I heard what he said. I heard him call me a nigger." Leonard's voice was smooth now, in control, calm. More, it was also tinged with sadness. He'd had more than three hours to think about things and decide what to do, and his emotions had run the gamut. "You know, Kevin, this isn't the first time I have been called a nigger by stupid whites. I knew they were just being mean and trying to lure me into a fight in order to prove that they were tough in front of their stupid friends. I have always felt out of place, been outnumbered since we've moved here. I have dealt with it by staying away from people like Matt. Their insults hurt, sure, but more than that, they just cut away at my hopes of fitting in at this school. I never had a best friend in school until you came along. And now I'm not so sure you're actually a friend." He added, "Just get out and leave me alone."

*There.* He'd said it. He'd said the words he had been rehearsing all morning.

Mouth agape, Kevin shook his head. "No, Leonard, you got it all wrong. I never called you that word, Matt did. I don't even believe in that kind of thing. You know that. You should have said something."

Abruptly Leonard's calm demeanor gave way to ire. He catapulted from the bed, took two quick steps, and shoved Kevin into the door.

Kevin offered no resistance nor did he attempt to stop Leonard. Though Kevin was being unjustly accused, he could see that his friend felt betrayed, hurt. He just wanted him to go back to being calm.

But no. As Kevin struggled to regain his balance and composure, Leonard raised his voice the loudest Kevin had ever heard it.

"No, Kevin!" Leonard shouted, his eyes filling with tears. "*You* should have said something! You should have stood up for me, had my back. But instead, you did nothing. I heard you do nothing. I bet after I left you never told him to stop calling me a nigger, did you? You see, there is a problem that you will never understand simply because of the color of your skin. That name Matt called me has been used forever to insult black people. It's used to supposedly keep us in our place; it's used to refer to us as something subhuman. It's used by people who think they are better than us simply because of their skin color. Maybe if you read a book every now and then, you'd know about all that."

Kevin started to say something, but Leonard was not finished. "Let me ask you a question, Kevin. Have you ever been called a name so repulsive that your anger and sadness are so huge that it surprises you? Scares you? I bet you have no idea. None."

Kevin tried hard to understand Leonard's point, but was taken back by the sheer fury that Leonard was showing toward him.

"Here, let me help you out. Let's try a few words. How about cracker, or whitee, or honkee, or maybe redneck? Oh wait, I got one more, white trash. That's the best I got, Kevin, a handful of insulting words. Not that bad? Does it conjure up any hatred in you at all? Does it make you angry the way I'm angry now?"

Fists in a ball, Leonard walked across the room to a large bookshelf that covered most of the wall under and around the sides of his window. Reaching up, he removed a book bound in hard, black leather. Kevin knew it was a book from his father's collection, cherished by Leonard because of its wisdom as much as its sentimental value. It was written by a black author, W. E. Burghardt Du Bois, entitled *Souls of Black Folk*. Leonard turned to a page marked with a black ribbon and read aloud to Kevin.

*"I remember well when the shadow swept across me. I was a little thing, away up in the hills of New England, where the dark Housatonic winds between Hoosac and Taghkanic to the sea. In a wee wooden schoolhouse, something put it into the boys' and girls' heads to buy gorgeous visiting-cards — ten cents a package — and exchange. The exchange was merry, till one girl, a tall newcomer, refused my card — refused it peremptorily, with a glance. Then it dawned upon me with a certain suddenness that I was different from the others; or like, mayhap, in heart and life and longing, but shut out from their world by a vast veil.*

"I found this quote marked in my father's book when I was eight, but I didn't understand what it meant until the first time someone called me a nigger." Leonard closed and returned the book to its place alongside many others on the shelf. He shot another look at Kevin. "I have one more question." He peered intently into Kevin's eyes. "Do you remember the first time someone called you a nigger?" He waited for the response he knew he would never hear.

"But I'm—"

"That's right," Leonard interrupted, "you're not black and you're definitely not a nigger, and neither am I."

Leonard backed away from Kevin and continued. "I'll share something with you, something you will never in your life experience. Something every black person encounters in their lives, usually when they're pretty young. It's the moment when we first feel our difference. It sticks in our heads forever. I remember that first time clearly, the pain of that word, always spoken out of hate. Just because I'm black and for *no other reason* than that."

Leonard turned and fell back onto the bed face down, exhausted, resigned. He grabbed his pillow with both hands and pulled it over his head. In a muffled voice from under the pillow, he made a final statement to Kevin.

"Someone who is my friend would never use that word or let someone else call me that word. You don't have the right. That word is a word of hatred, and if you are my friend, it shouldn't be a part of us. Now go away, Kevin, and leave me alone."

Kevin drew in a deep breath, slow and long, until he could take in no more, then held it as he decided what to do. He didn't want things to end this way, but he also didn't understand much of what was happening and didn't know what to do. He struggled with his thoughts, then let go of that deep breath, equally slow and long. If there was anything he could do, he couldn't see it. His chin tucked and his lips quivered as tears welled up in his eyes. He suddenly felt very lost in this once-familiar place. He turned to leave. He missed the door handle on his first reach for it. The room had changed: the walls shifted and the floor tilted to one side. The words of his best friend transmitted the finality of their relationship. He left the door to Leonard's room open as he headed into the hall, where he bumped into Leonard's mom, who shuffled him to the living room. She hugged Kevin.

"It's okay, child. He is still your friend. The two of you will work this out, and all will be right as rain. He didn't mean what he said. Just give it a little time."

It was obvious that Lynette had been listening on the other side of the door. But her words brought little comfort, especially when he heard Leonard slam the door to his room.

The conversation with Leonard replayed repeatedly in his head, as did Matt's taunts.

"What happened?" he said aloud as he walked home. "How did Leonard think I called him a nigger when it was Matt that said it and not me? What did I do wrong?" No matter how hard he tried, he could not find fault in his actions. But there was a thought creeping in on him, and it made him uncomfortable.

Had he been a coward? Should he have told Matt to leave him alone and demanded that he not refer to his friend in that horrid way? But if he'd done that, he may have set Matt off, and he could have gotten hurt. Matt would welcome any reason to fight, especially someone younger and weaker. Matt was the poster child for bullies. Kevin had been afraid Matt would hurt him if he objected.

Coward?

# 29

When Kevin arrived home, his mother and father were halfway through cutting the grass. Normally the grass cutting and yard work was done on Saturdays, but this was a special day because of the Fourth of July weekend, and his parents had Friday off as well as Monday. Jane used the riding mower, and Allen pushed away with a small mower in order to cut between the trees and small shrubs carefully placed in the front yard. They had enhanced the landscaping since they'd moved in, adding splendid accents to the lush, green St. Augustine. The front yard stretched out along their oyster-shell driveway and touched the edges of the main dirt road after gently rising up from the drainage ditch at the end of the yard.

"Hey, working man," his father said as he reached out and rubbed Kevin's head. He was sweaty and shirtless. Even in the early morning sun, it was already warming up, a prelude to the blazes that would beat down on them as the day progressed.

"How was work?" Allen asked.

"Fine," Kevin replied, obviously somber.

His father quickly picked up on the mood in Kevin's voice, but he really had no time to dig further into it right then. The yard had to be finished before the brutality of the noonday sun scorched the ambition to finish the job.

"Fine, huh?" Allen said, just to make sure his instinct was correct. It was.

"Dad, I need to talk to you about something. It's really important."

"Is it about to explode, catch on fire, or cause a train wreck in the next hour?" his dad asked.

"No, not really," Kevin admitted, his voice heavy, barely heard over the sound of the lawnmower.

"Good. Here, take over the push mower for me so I can get the trimmer going. Oh, it needs gas," Allen said as he headed for the utility shed behind the house.

"But Dad, I really want to talk to you," Kevin said.

"Can it wait until we finish the yard?"

Normally a response of "fine" from Kevin would have drawn his father in to ask more questions about his day. However, the rush was apparently on to complete the yard work, and there would be no time at the present for extended conversation about the word "fine."

Kevin conceded, nodding his head. "Yeah, it can wait, I guess."

The next hour of yard work was agonizing for Kevin on many levels. Besides the heat, his head was overrun with questions he could not answer by himself. He needed his dad's opinion to finally end this annoying nagging in his head. He pushed aggressively at the mower and tried to think of other things, but he was hopelessly consumed with worry. He needed the guidance of someone far wiser than he to help sort out the tangled mess that he'd suddenly become a part of.

Finally, the yard work was done. Everyone had showered and changed and was ready to relax in the oak grove at the back of the house. Allen leaned back in a comfortable lawn chair in the beloved shade and said, "Okay boy, what's on your mind? I can tell something is bugging you by the way you took it out on that poor, helpless lawn mower. I bet you knocked the bark off of every one of your mother's pear trees."

Kevin smiled, thinking, *Where do I start?*

The low branches hung heavy with green leaves, inviting what little breezes there might be in the air to drop by for a visit. The oak grove backed up to the Kelso Ranch. Four thin strands of barbed wire nailed to mesquite and cedar posts separated Kevin's backyard from the ranch property. A short distance away, the calm waters of Clear Creek flowed gently to its eventual destination of the Gulf of Mexico. Kevin settled into a lawn chair, fiddling with the tendrils on his cutoffs. His mother had just emerged from the back door and was carrying a tray of cold drinks.

"Uh, wait. Is it okay if your mother's in on this conversation, or is this just guy talk?" Allen asked. Jane's eyebrows went up inquisitively.

"No, I think Mom can help with this one. It's sort of complicated," Kevin replied.

"Complicated, huh?" Jane said, handing each of them a drink. "What are you boys up to?"

"I believe we are about to begin a complicated conversation that you can probably help with," Allen said as he leaned forward, ready to tackle the conundrum head on.

Over the course of the next half hour, Kevin revealed his story of that morning's events to his parents. He tried not to leave out any detail, including what Matt said, what Leonard heard, what Kevin did and did not do, and going to Leonard's house. He confessed how worried he'd been when Leonard hadn't shown up and then how surprised he'd been at Leonard's anger toward him. He said he wondered if he should have done something different and that he didn't know what to do now. His concerns were simple really; he just wanted his friend back.

"Son, it sounds like, from what you're telling me, Leonard has a valid reason for being angry with you. You did not stand up for him, and from what Leonard heard, it was enough to convince him that you could not be counted on to stand up for him when there was an injustice being done toward him," Jane said, always the blunt one.

Kevin turned to his father, who had been listening intently

to his story. He waited for the wise words of Allen Ferris to be delivered. But his dad offered no suggestions nor did he expound on the comments Jane had just made.

So Jane continued, talking about how friends should look out for one another and how it wasn't right to tolerate poor talk about another person, especially a friend. Of course, this was not the answer Kevin was looking for. Then his mother went one step further into the "not what I'm looking for" category by suggesting that he tell Mr. Kelso about Matt's behavior. It seemed Kevin's situation was just getting worse instead of better.

"No way, Mom. Matt would beat the tar out of me if I say anything to anyone!" His voice was high and panicked as he tried to explain to his mother about that certain code between boys that you just don't break.

Jane countered that Matt was more of a man than a boy and that Kevin should definitely speak to Mr. Kelso about what was going on.

Kevin laughed doubtfully. "Well, I may not be a man, but Matt will sure hit me like a man if I said anything to Mr. Kelso."

Kevin once again turned to his father, hoping for some masculine backup. He was deep in thought and looked almost disconnected from the conversation.

Having said all she wanted to say about the situation, Jane picked up the empty tray and glasses, which were quickly drained, to bring refills from the house. Before she left, she paused in front of Allen, giving him the not-so-subtle look that it was time for a man's point of view.

Allen held back his comments until Jane was in the house and had closed the door. The pause was long and awkward for Kevin. *Does everything have to be so intense?*

In the fig tree next to the garage, a mockingbird began his afternoon serenade, along with the soothing sound of the breeze blowing through the leaves of the trees. For now, that was all that filled the silence ringing in Kevin's impatient ears.

When his father finally spoke up, it was not at all what Kevin thought he would say.

"Son," Allen started in a low, even voice. "We moved from Houston to get away from the crowds and the traffic. Most of all, we moved to get you away from the school you were in. We heard many bad things that were going on there, and we didn't want you exposed to them. I am sorry we took you away from your friends and especially your swim team, but we really felt it was the best thing for you. We still do. We found this school and think it's a good one for you."

"You mean it's good because it was mostly white kids?" Kevin asked.

"I guess in a way that was part of our thinking. And if it was, we were wrong. You did a good job of navigating through any problems at your old school, and you probably would have continued to do so. Still, as parents we have to consider many aspects of what's best for the family. I am sorry we jerked your life up by the roots, but I'm convinced it will strengthen you for the long haul. That's my job, to get you there."

"I get that, Dad. And I like it here. I've made a lot of friends during school this year. I am even thinking about trying out for the baseball team."

Allen's eyes lit up at that possibility. "Now that's what I wanted to hear," he said, leaning over to place his hand on his son's shoulder and grasp it firmly, encouragingly.

Another pause.

"I have never seen you happier than you are in this place. I watch you play in Mr. Kelso's fields with Leonard, and you take me with you, in spirit, every time you go," Allen said. "When I watch the two of you boldly run with your fishing poles and bare backs into your next adventure, I'm right there with you. Just thinking about you enjoying your life like that, pure and simple, makes me rest a little easier at night. My days don't drag down with worry for you anymore. In Houston, you played on concrete with buildings as far as the eye could see.

Now the grassy fields and creek beds are your playgrounds. At the end of the day, you and Leonard come home with briar scratches, mosquito bites, skinned knees, and smiles that can be seen as bright as sunshine through your mud-covered faces. The best part is I get to live a little of your childhood too."

Kevin's father stopped and this time put his hand on his son's head, gently. "Seeing you grow up here makes me happy, and Leonard is part of that happiness. Son, you have to make things right with him. If what you are telling me is true about this fella Matt and what he said, I have to take your mother's position in general. Still she doesn't realize, I suspect, what you and I both know. You let the fear of being hurt stop you from standing up for your best friend."

Kevin squirmed, frowned at the ground.

"Don't let your fears override your reasoning. A black eye worn by an honorable person can be displayed with pride. Sometimes you will have to fight for the right thing—that is something every gentleman of good character knows and something a boy learns as he turns into a man. You are at a threshold in your life, son, and it makes me proud that you would ask for my advice as to how to cross it."

Perplexed, Kevin looked up at his dad and replied, "So, you want me to fight Matt? He's, like, ten times bigger than me, Dad! He drives a car. He even shaves! He'll pummel me in a fight! I heard he got kicked out of school because he *killed a tenth-grader!*"

Allen laughed at that one. "Now that's not true and you know it; you're exaggerating. What I'm trying to tell you is this: stand up to him, stand up for your friend. Sometimes doing the right thing may cost you a few bumps and lumps, but trust me, there's no shame in that. Get your friend back and make things right again. Make it right so the two of you don't miss another day of these great days in your young life. There will come a day when the two of you won't have time to cross that barbed wire fence and go fishing. Adult life just gets in the way. So build those memories now, so you have something to pull from when you're older. Don't screw it up because you didn't do the right thing today."

That did it. The pieces fell together for Kevin into a complete picture. He finally understood what his father—and his mother—were getting at.

He sat for a moment, allowing himself to face his fear of Matt and weigh that fear against losing his best friend. The first thought that clamored in his head now was to go to Leonard and confess his mistakes and promise to never let it happen again. He sprung from his chair as if he were launched from a cannon.

"Whoa, where do you think you're going?"

"To Leonard's house. I've got to talk to him right now, Dad," Kevin explained.

"Whoa, whoa. Sit down, son," Allen said, holding his hands up to stop Kevin. "Son, that's not the right thing, not right now. Leonard needs time to think, and so do you. Now, let this go until Leonard is ready to talk again. He'll let you know."

"But Dad, it has already been almost four hours. That's plenty of time for him to think about it. Don't you think?"

The back door slammed, and they looked up. Jane was on her way out with a tray full of fresh drinks and slices of watermelon. She started down the steps of the back porch. Their two dogs Tripper and Sammy were in close pursuit.

"I'll tell you what we'll do; first let's enjoy the refreshments your mother is bringing us, then we'll ask her advice. If she agrees with you, you can run down to Leonard's after we eat. If she agrees with me, well then, that's two against one and you really should take our advice. Deal?"

Kevin took a deep breath and tried his best to suppress the urge to jump up and run. Of course, he quickly reminded himself, hadn't he come to his parents for advice?

"That's a dirty trick to play on a kid, Dad. I know how this is going to turn out."

"It's going to turn out for the best, boy."

The discussion was short, and all agreed that it would be best to sit back and allow Leonard time to decompress. Kevin and his family enjoyed the remainder of the day in a comfortable breeze that blew in from the pasture and across Clear Creek. It wasn't every day when the path to forgiveness could be mapped out and anticipated. But today had been one of those for Kevin.

# 30

This was going to be the worst weekend of Kevin's life. He would be spending Saturday without his friend, and then Sunday would come crashing down on him. It would be a day spent at church until around noon—a torturous hour and a half spent in uncomfortable clothing and even more uncomfortable seating. Then would come another hour after that of socializing with grownups and listening to friends of his parents repeating the same old spiel: *Kevin, you are growing so tall. Kevin, don't you look handsome! Kevin, how are you liking it here so far?* There would even be the occasional pinch on the cheek, and almost everyone polished their palms on his stubbly, shaven head.

*What a total waste of a perfect day. I could be fishing. I could be having fun! Agh!*

After church, Kevin plopped on his bed, good clothes laying in a pile on the floor. He knew he would have to hang them up, but he defiantly wanted them to suffer on the carpet for a few minutes more. He could only agonize over the future socializing that was still to take place, either at church, or at someone's house; he didn't even remember what the plan was supposed to be today. And he didn't care. All he could think about was running with Leonard, wearing worn-out clothes, dirty old shoes, and fishing tackle clanking at their sides.

The only good thing about Sundays in summer was when, after dinner, he and Leonard could go for a jaunt, since the light lasted for hours.

And he needed a head shave. This popped into his head for no reason, except that he was thinking about all the things he and Leonard would do during their short reprieve on Sunday evenings. Leonard's mother would sometimes set the boys up on the back porch to "tune up their haircuts," as she liked to call it. A few quick seconds of electric tremors and they were left with a cool and tidy neckline.

He remembered how he and Leonard had planned for buzz cuts this summer. With a tablecloth wrapped around their necks, Lynette set the trimmers to buzz and sheared the hairs from their heads so that only nubs were left. On the back porch floor boards, Kevin's brown locks mixed with Leonard's tight curls. It had surprised them how much hair had come off them, and they'd palmed their heads curiously. The sensation of a bald head to a young boy in the Texas sun enhanced the feeling of freedom, or so it seemed.

Sunday slowly crept by and gave way to Monday, the Fourth of July. Kevin's family had no major plans for the holiday, except to go to a friend's house in Houston for an early dinner and to enjoy some fireworks later on that evening. Instead of sleeping in and waiting to leave, Kevin woke at five o'clock and dressed, planning to make his way to the ranch. His father, normally an early bird, was already up. A steaming pile of eggs and a big bowl of grits were on the table. This was new.

"Breakfast of champs. Want some?" Allen offered.

"No thanks, Dad," Kevin said in a sleepy voice.

"I thought you had the weekend off?" His father asked.

"I do, but—"

"Ah. Never mind. I think I get it." Kevin's father understood. His son was holding out hope that perhaps today Leonard would return to work, a neutral ground where they could talk. "But you better hurry before your mother wakes up and talks you out of it."

Kevin grinned and swiftly moved through the house and out the door.

# 31

Kevin pushed his way through the barbed wire fence, gently spreading the wires and placing his legs through one at a time. It was easy and fast without the burden of fishing poles, tackle boxes, and sacks of lunch. Walking in the early morning through a cow pasture could be a hazardous venture, as Kevin was all too aware, so he walked with care. Ant hills were sometimes as high as his ankles, and cow pies were sure things to avoid, the fresh ones especially. Today he was particularly intent on these things, trying to keep his mind busy.

On occasion, he would look up and scan the land around him, hoping to see Leonard also on his way to work. Most days, he could easily spot Leonard walking in the same direction — but not this morning. A little hope remained that perhaps Leonard had already gotten to work and was there, waiting. Kevin wasn't sure what he would say when he confronted him, so he came up with a plan: he would just act casual and keep his mouth shut until Leonard made the first move at conversation. At least he would try.

———•———

Clint stood at the far end of the barn, turning on the light switches one by one as the horses impatiently stomped, demanding their breakfast. He then removed his cowboy hat and began rubbing his head, reading the chalkboard itinerary for the morning. As was usually the case, at the top of the list was a request for Whisky by the Drink to be saddled and ready for a ride.

He turned when he heard Kevin's approach and watched

him in silence as the boy walked the lighted stretch between the stalls. He noticed the boy checking the shadows of each stall—probably to make sure Matt was not creeping around somewhere. Or maybe he was looking for his buddy Leonard.

"You know you had today off, right?" Clint asked, looking at Kevin with a lifted brow.

"Yes sir, but it's kind of boring around the house."

Clint gazed down at him and knew something was wrong; however, instead of asking and harping on it, maybe making things worse, he decided to go with a diversion.

"Well, since you're here, I may as well put you to work. The stalls will be fine today—they don't need cleaning. So, you can help me saddle Whisky. Do you know where Whisky's tack is, boy?" Clint asked in his slow, gritty drawl.

"Tack?" Kevin asked, confused.

"Yes, boy, tack. You know, saddle, bridle, and blanket."

"Yes sir. It's in the room full of saddles."

"That's right, boy. We call that room the tack room. You can't miss it. There's a sign above the door that says 'Tack Room.' And that's where saddles, bridles, and blankets—all the horse gear—is kept. It's tack." Clint was having a little fun with his young friend, spilling out playful sarcasm, though he wasn't sure Kevin was catching on. "Now be sure you fetch the right tack for Mr. Kelso's horse. You can't miss it; it's hung on the saddle horse below a placard that says 'Whisky by the Drink.' Bring it to me, and I'll show you how to saddle a horse."

———◆———

Kevin felt privileged to perform a task that Clint usually did himself. The saddle was heavy, and the aroma of the polished leather was strong but pleasant as he carried it over to Whisky's stall and set it down on a small table just outside of it. The table had a half round section of boards built into the top of it, so that the saddle sat upon it and did not touch the ground. It took Kevin three trips to retrieve all the necessary tack in order to prepare Whisky for his morning ride. When that job was complete, Clint told him to get started feeding the horses—all the feed and hay was already laid out—and then he would show Kevin the proper way to bridle and saddle Whisky.

They had just finished feeding the last of the horses when Matt drove up. Clint expressed his discontent for Matt's usual tardiness with a slight grunt. As Matt entered the barn, he walked past Kevin, who was closing the stall door of the last horse he'd fed. Kevin's eyes stayed looking in any direction that did not include Matt.

"Matt!" Clint barked from across the barn. "Get down here and then take this wheelbarrow out back to feed all the goats."

"Goats! Don't you think that's a job for the greenhorn?"

"The greenhorn was on time, even though he didn't have to come into work today; you're not. That gives you goat duty."

Matt picked up the wheelbarrow and pushed it to the back of the barn so he could fill it with goat feed.

As he passed by Kevin, he asked in a low, snaky voice, "Where is your little friend this morning?"

Kevin ignored him and walked away, heading for the next task to be done, whatever that was, even if it was just getting away from Matt. He wished Clint was still out there. He had stepped inside the tack room and could not hear nor see the conversation between Matt and Kevin.

"You must be deaf. Every time I ask you something, you don't answer back. Now where is your little friend at?"

Silence.

"Ohhhh," Matt said with exaggerated realization, "I bet he's out there in the dark somewhere. That's why I can't see him."

More silence, but this time Kevin's tension was evident. *No more,* he thought to himself. *I cannot put up with this anymore.*

He could feel the frustration build in him like pressure in a can of soda that had just been kicked across the ground. And Matt was pulling back the tab.

Chin set firmly, Kevin tried to force back the din growing in his mind. Though he tried his best, he knew it would ultimately be futile. Matt would keep pushing him, and he would explode.

With obvious disgust, Kevin spat out, "Geez, shut up, Matt! I didn't answer you back because I don't want to answer you back. I don't even want to talk to you. Leave me alone."

Just then, Kevin could see Clint emerging from the tack room, a wide brush in hand. But he was still far enough away to be unaware of the brewing exchange. Matt casually began pushing the wheelbarrow out the back of the barn, passing Kevin with a low, wicked snicker.

*He sure is pleased with himself,* Kevin thought. Matt's only goal in life seemed to be to annoy and draw blood.

"Good morning, boy."

Kevin wheeled around, startled.

"Did you enjoy your weekend? I thought you had today off as well?" Bo asked, emerging from the outside shadows and into the light of the barn.

It was then Kevin understood Matt's sudden retreat. Bullies had a sixth sense when it came to people in positions of authority, a built-in warning system—like fine, little hairs on the back of their necks—that tells them: it's time to play the nice guy and save the game for later.

———•———

Bo cocked his head to the side, chin tilted up slightly to get a better view of Kevin's face. What he saw, he could not completely fathom: the pain of a shattered friendship, the frustration with a barn bully, and the loneliness of it all. Even in the darkest shadows of the barn, Kevin's worry was as visible as the rising sun, sneaking into the sky. Bo didn't know details, but he had an inkling. He kept it to himself for now.

"Is Leonard here yet?" Kevin's voice had a high pitch to it.

"Nope, I don't think he's coming back to work. His mother called me the other day and told me that he didn't want to work here anymore." He eyed Kevin. "I may be an old man, but I know when there is noise in the henhouse. Something's wrong."

Kevin's eyes scanned the fading darkness over the pasture as the sun pushed its way into the morning sky. The yawning rays of the sun were a brilliant red and orange. Bo knew he was searching the pasture for his friend. Sensing Kevin's reluctance to talk, he placed his hand on the young man's shoulder and guided him and Whisky out of the barn. A few feet outside the barn, he tied Whisky to a hitching post. It was made of cedar, a little more than four inches thick and stretched across two larger cedar legs, buried firmly in the ground. Each end of the six-foot-long cedar hitching post had a four-inch-wide copper band that molded around the cedar like a glove and attached the post to the upright legs.

"Here, boy. Let me show you the first knot I ever learned to tie."

Bo took Whisky's reins, looped them around the post two times, and then back under. The two flat sections of leather were perfectly aligned side by side and locked together. He then gave them a firm tug to show there was no give.

"My father taught me that knot, after he handed me the reins of my first horse; I never forgot it. He only showed me that knot one time. Even over the excitement of receiving such a grand gift, it didn't distract me from memorizing that knot." Cryptically, he finished, "Funny, the things we remember, the things we are taught and don't forget, even though there are some things we would like to forget."

They stood leaning over the hitching post, Kevin on one side and Bo on the other with Whisky a step back. Whisky's sleepy, brown eyes drooped as his long eyelashes flickered in an attempt to stay awake.

"Did you and your friend have some sort of fight?"

"Something like that. Leonard thinks I called him a name." Kevin paused for only a moment before the entire story came pouring out, smooth and honest, like a pitcher of cold water.

Bo nodded throughout the narrative, taking in every word

without interrupting or offering advice. Even Whisky was patient, waiting for his morning ride as he arched one of his back legs in a resting posture. When Kevin had emptied his heart, Bo offered only one bit of advice: "I think your parents are right. You should give it time. It will work itself out."

"But what if it doesn't?" Kevin asked.

Bo reached out with his thumb and forefinger and gently pulled at the two leather straps draped on top of one another. They slipped off the hitching post and made a slapping sound as they flipped off the railing. Lifting his left hand up, both straps landed cleanly in his palm.

"Boy, there ain't a knot in this world that can't be untied."

Kevin stared at the reins draped across the old man's palm, astonished at how easily he'd removed them from the hitching post.

"You just got to know which end of the rope to untie first."

With that, Bo placed his left foot in the stirrup, grasped the saddle horn, and swung a leg over Whisky's back.

"Take your parents' advice, son. This knot will untie itself."

———— • ————

Kevin watched Whisky, his boss astride, move into the brightening face of day as the sun rose over the banks of Clear Creek.

"Oh that's just great, more advice I can't use," Kevin said to no one in particular. Then he had a more distressing revelation; Matt was headed in his direction.

Kevin stepped to the side to give Matt plenty of reeking room, the unmistakable combination of cigarettes and beer strong.

"Well?" Matt blurted out as he passed, poking Kevin in the shoulder.

Enveloped in his own concerns, Kevin was in no mood for scare tactics or Matt's mouth. He had spent his long weekend without his friend, without fishing, without good feelings in general. Kevin and Leonard had made grand plans for this weekend—which did not include work, parents, or household chores—to bask in the summer sun on the banks of Clear Creek or one of the many water tanks, fishing and cutting up. As Kevin looked at Matt now, he saw only the person who had messed that all up for him and Leonard.

He snapped.

"Well what?!" Kevin shouted back, taking an aggressive step forward.

"Whoa. Someone is in a cranky mood this morning."

"Stay away from me, Matt."

Matt's eyes took on a whole new level of squint.

"Hey!" Clint called out from the other end of the barn. "Get out there and clean the goat bedding, Matt."

"Let the spook feed them when he gets here; he's obviously later than I am."

"Shut your mouth, Matt!" Kevin's hands were outstretched and rigid behind him with the force of his command.

Faster than either of them could anticipate, Clint was already halfway down the hall of the barn, arms swinging, boots stomping in long strides, *heel toe heel toe*. Clearly Clint had reached his boiling point.

"I've had enough of you two. I came to work in a good mood this morning because I had the barn all to myself for couple of days. If the two of you start up again, I'll send you home for an extended vacation. Now get to your work so I can get rid of you and have the barn quiet and to myself again. Horses are far better company than two arguing children. Tend to the goats, Matt."

"That's not fit work for a cowboy, and you know it, Clint; it's greenhorn duty."

"No, it's your duty for showing up late again. Besides that, you're no cowboy." Clint stepped close so Matt could see his eyes in the shadows of his cowboy hat. Then he angled forward, his long, lean frame towering over Matt. "And that's *Mr. Clint* to you, boy."

He dragged out his words as he said them, so Matt understood without question who was in charge. Matt offered no challenge or response. He looked into Clint's eyes just long enough to see the left one twitch and realized this cowboy was not playing around. Clint turned and walked out of the barn past Kevin, who stood like a statue, taking it all in. Kevin walked back to the stall he was cleaning. Clint had set things right, at least for now.

Peace restored, no matter if temporarily, Kevin finished cleaning the stalls. He then went to the building where the sacks of feed were kept and loaded his wheelbarrow with the eighty-pound burlap sacks. Matt finished feeding the goats, then was instructed by Clint to help Kevin with the sacks of feed. The adversaries worked together in silence, each hauling the sacks one at a time into the barn via wheelbarrow. Meanwhile, Clint had removed one of the mares and brushed her in the middle of the barn, where he could observe all the goings-on both inside and out. He figured by the time they had recharged the feed bins, the boys would be too tired to fight. However, that was not to be the case.

Unable to restrain from his needling ways, Matt picked up where he'd left off. He pulled up to Kevin at the pile of feed sacks, breaking the silence as he reached for another bag of feed.

"So, where is your little friend today? Work too tough for him?"

"Shut your face, Matt."

Matt leaned in close as Kevin wrapped his hands around a bag of feed. "Look, you little runt. I don't put up with anyone talking to me like that, let alone a little sawed-off squirt like you."

Kevin lifted his sack onto the front half of his wheelbarrow, preparing to flip the rest of it over, when he saw Matt heading in his direction, sackless. One step, two steps, and on the third step, just as Matt was reaching for Kevin's T-shirt over the wheelbarrow, Kevin flipped the sack with all his power.

The weight of the sack turned the wheelbarrow onto its side and Matt's feet. As the momentum of the sack's forward motion continued, it rolled out of the wheelbarrow completely and knocked Matt backward between the two barrels. The full weight of the sack was on his legs, pinning Matt to the ground.

Spastically trying to free himself from the mess, Matt screamed, "I'm going to bust your head open, you little turd!"

Kevin jumped back from the tangled mess of feed bags and wheelbarrows. From that vantage point, only Matt's bobbing head and one waving arm was discernible in the pile. By the time Matt had untangled himself from the mess, Kevin was ready. He stood with both his hands up in a boxing stance as Matt stepped over the second wheelbarrow and swung wildly at Kevin, the swoosh of air from Matt's errant swing causing Kevin to slam his eyes shut as he flinched in anticipation of the impact of Matt's fist.

Kevin suddenly recalled his boxing lessons with Mr. Flowers. The former boxer had told him, "You have to keep your eyes open and your hands up. If you see the punch coming, your eyes will tell your feet to move your body and your head. So protect, watch, and move."

Opening his eyes, Kevin moved his feet to the left, sidestepping Matt's next swing and then the next. Finally Matt got his feet under him and was now toe-to-toe with Kevin.

*This can't be good,* Kevin thought. He almost preferred Matt to take swings at him.

After three missed attempts to connect with Kevin, Matt charged. Kevin quickly stepped to one side again, knocking Matt's hand away with his left arm. Matt spun halfway around, and as he regained his balance and turned, Kevin struck him square on the nose with a left jab and a quick right.

*Oh my God! I hit him!* To Kevin's utter astonishment, Matt

fell backward, tripping over one of the wheelbarrow handles, then landing with great impact on his butt.

*What have I done? He's going to really kill me now.*

Although Kevin had been able to connect with Matt's face—Kevin was a head shorter—the statistics were on Matt's side. Short of Kevin picking up a pitchfork, Matt would be the victor at the end of this fight.

Matt reached up and felt his nose. When he pulled his hand down, it was full of blood. His eyes widened and his entire face wrinkled up like a gorilla's. Kevin was horrified as Matt jumped to his feet. For a brief second, Kevin thought about running, but there was no time. He tried to sidestep Matt once again, but Matt latched onto him this time and hung on fiercely, forcing him to fall backward to the ground. Now underneath Matt, Kevin grabbed for his arm and wrenched it away. The good news was that it worked. The bad news was that it took both of his hands to release Matt's grip. That was to Matt's advantage because he hit Kevin in the left eye with his other hand. As he drew back his hand to lay out another hit, Kevin let go of Matt's arm in order to cover his face, and . . .

It was over?

Matt was gone. He didn't feel Matt's weight on top of him anymore. He opened his eyes between the slits of his fingers and lifted his head to see Clint standing over him and Matt well into his second somersault.

———•———

Clint had gotten there just in time to grab the arm Matt had cocked back like a loaded jackhammer. With one arm, Clint had flung the troublemaker off Kevin, like a blanket from a horse's back. When Matt stopped tumbling, he came to rest just in front of the barn door—directly in front of Bo Kelso's feet. Bo had emerged from the barn, Whisky's reins in hand, just in time to witness the final act. The last thing he expected to see was his ranch hands in the middle of a dusty brawl.

"You boys out of things to do?" Bo asked calmly, mildly amused.

Matt struggled to his feet, and fast. Clint helped Kevin to his feet, and the two fighters took a few minutes to assess their damages.

"Did you see that?" Clint asked, as he entered the barn and stood next to Bo.

"See what?"

"Matt's bloody nose. Kevin gave it to him. That kid really put it on him."

Bo slowly shook his head, thinking, a smirk peeping out of the corner of his mouth. He called the boys over.

"I can't have you boys fighting." He scanned their faces. They were both somber and quiet. Bo reached out with his left hand, turned Kevin's chin to one side, and examined his eye. He then directed his attention toward Matt's still-bleeding nose.

"If the two of you can't get along, I'll have to fire both of you."

The boys simultaneously spoke up in protest, promising they would be able to get along.

"We were just playing around, Mr. Kelso. It sort of got out of hand, that's all," Matt said.

Bo stared intently at Matt's bleeding nose and then turned back to Kevin to take notice of his quickly swelling eye. He shook his head and, without saying another word, tied Whisky's reins to the hitching post before walking back through the barn.

Clint retrieved a handful of ice cubes from the small refrigerator in his office. Wrapping them in a small towel, he handed it to Kevin and instructed him to hold it on his eye in order to stop the swelling. He did the same for Matt. A short time later, he sent both duelling ranch hands home.

# 32

By the time Kevin arrived back at his house, Allen had already heard about the showdown. Bo had called ahead as a courtesy, apologizing for what he called "a barnyard squabble."

Waiting impatiently on the back porch for Kevin to arrive, Allen explained again to Jane what the rancher had told him. As Kevin neared the fence, his mother could barely contain her worry. She started across the porch to assess her son's damage, but Allen held her back: "You can't treat him like that. You'll make him feel like a little boy, and he is no longer one."

Allen knew she saw the wisdom in this, though she maybe didn't like it much. To her credit, she managed to keep her fussing to a bare minimum when Kevin hit the porch with a swollen eye, but broader shoulders. Allen noticed a difference in his son's walk—he stood taller, his shoulders wider, a swagger now evident.

*Now that's the walk of a confident man,* the proud father thought. He knew his son had just taken a huge step in the direction of manhood today. Instinctively, Allen wanted so desperately to hear every detail of the fight. But he knew now wasn't the right time, if ever. Working his demeanor into one of authority, he set aside the morbid curiosity that goes with such an event and approached his son.

# 33

"Good morning." Bo tipped his hat, sitting tall atop Whisky.

"And a good morning to you, sir," Lynette Parker politely replied.

She and Leonard sat on a long wooden bench under the eave of their back porch in the morning shade. They had just finished breakfast and were enjoying a glass of iced tea. A curly-haired, blonde girl emerged from the back door holding a serving jug of tea; a small, white-lace napkin was draped over her left arm. She was playing the part of hostess at what she considered a high-brow tea party. When she saw Bo perched atop Whisky at the back fence, she spoke up in an overly polite tone, "Will the gentleman be joining us for tea?"

Bo caught the eye roll from Leonard and realized that this must be the infamous Jenny that he and Kevin had spoken of. Jenny gave Bo a look of exacerbated tolerance. "You'll have to park your animal in the pasture; we do not serve horses at tea."

Leonard's mother smiled and giggled softly at Jenny's request.

"Why, thank you, ma'am, but I won't be attending tea this morning. However, I do appreciate your hospitality." Bo reached up for his hat brim, removed his hat from his head, and placed it across his chest. He bowed. "I would like a word with Master Leonard; however, if this is not a good time, I can return later."

Bo easily stepped into the role of guest at Jenny's high-brow party. She responded in kind with a curtsy.

"Very well then. Mrs. Parker, shall we retire to the kitchen and give the gentlemen some privacy?"

"Why certainly, my dear; we do have dishes to tend to, after all. We'll just leave you gentlemen to the backyard."

Leonard's mother entered the back door and made her way to the kitchen, as Leonard walked across the backyard up to the barbed wire fence, where Bo sat on his horse.

Bo spoke first. "I was wondering if you forgot your way to work." He paused, waiting for a response, and received none. "Well, I know your mother called me and said you weren't coming back to work. I figured you had her call." He waited again for a response, which did not come. Leonard was digging his toes into the grass, not daring to look up. "Unfortunately, that's not the way it goes. I need to hear it from you. I didn't hire your mother; I hired you, and when a man quits his job, he tells the boss in person."

Leonard appeared to have great difficulty lifting his head to look Bo in the eye. He drew in a ragged breath and let it out before he started to speak. His words came slowly, almost inaudible at first. "No sir . . . I really . . . don't want to quit. I guess I just needed a little time to think."

"You mean ruminate—that's far more intense than just thinking," Bo replied.

"Ruminate?" Leonard asked.

"Ruminate. In cowboy lingo, that means you're doing something at the same time you're thinking about something, so your chances of solving the problem are far greater. I reckon you're ruminating on who your friends are."

"Yes sir, that's basically what I'm doing," Leonard replied.

"I suppose you heard we had a little bullfight go on at the barn the other day?"

"Yes sir, I heard about it," Leonard said, squinting his eyes against the sun rising behind Bo atop his horse. Lynette had heard the story earlier from Jane Ferris.

"Yep, I reckon you did." Bo paused and allowed the moment to soak. "You know that boy who you weren't too sure was your friend took a pretty good lick for you. He's got a shiner the size of the dish plate because he stood up. He stood up for himself, and in doing so, he stood up for you too."

Leonard nodded his head and then looked down at his feet again, kicked at the grass.

"Kevin made a decision that will define him for the rest of his life. He raised his chin before his fist, and in doing that, he crossed a threshold that will lead him into manhood. Now I'm not pointing my finger in any particular direction," Bo said, "but I think this would have turned out a whole lot better if the two of you had stood up together at the first sign of trouble. Kevin felt like a coward that morning, but not for the reason you think. He felt that way because of you and the way you treated him at your house. You turned and ran home. Was it because Kevin wouldn't take up for you or was it because you were also afraid of Matt?"

Bo continued, not waiting for a response. "Either way, it was you that set these events into motion. Kevin came back and faced Matt. He faced his fears, and he is stronger for it. He even came back and faced you, seeking your understanding and forgiveness. You have Kevin all twisted up inside like a triple knot in a thin, leather strap, thinking he did something wrong, when the truth is all he did was protect himself by not saying anything, *just like you did.*" Bo said the last words slower and louder for extra emphasis.

Leonard looked up at his old friend, this time holding his eyes on him.

"Son, barbed wire cuts on both sides of the fence. I reckon you'll need to patch things up before you cut yourself so deeply it won't heal." Bo paused and leaned forward in the saddle, his left elbow on the saddle horn and his right hand perched across it, holding Whisky's reins. The shadow of his cowboy hat and shoulders were outlined on the grass by Leonard's feet. The conversation grew quiet as both of them gathered their thoughts.

Whisky's ears flickered, and he lowered his head to pluck the grass from the ground at Leonard's feet. The boy reached out his hand and rubbed Whisky's mane as the sound of his jaws grinding the sweet, green blades punctuated the silence.

"The friendship the two of you share is far stronger than Matt's shallow stupidity. You see, in a way Matt is pathetic because of his ignorance. He bullies weaker people to make himself feel better about the way he is. He is that way because that is all he has ever known or chooses to know."

Leonard understood what Bo was telling him, but he wasn't sure where he was going with it. So he listened intently and made eye contact with Bo over Whisky's head.

"The fact is that Matt would've found a way to give you and Kevin a hard time no matter what color the two of you were. That's just what fellows like Matt do. Do you understand?"

"I think so." There was a slight question in Leonard's response and then he asked, "Did Kevin come back to work today?"

"Yes sir, he did," Bo answered.

"Well, I don't like Matt."

"That's okay; I don't like him much either."

"Yeah, but you are bigger than he is, and you can fire him if you wanted to."

"I reckon I could. However, even a fellow like Matt needs a place to fit in. If I fired everyone I didn't get along with, the work would never get done. And I am too old to do it all myself. Besides that, you have to figure there are goat ropers and bullies leaning against every fence post in every pasture you will cross in your lifetime. You may as well learn to deal with them now.

"What's more important here is your friendship with Kevin. I think the two of you together can wrangle Matt easy enough. If I fire Matt, he'll just go somewhere else and stir up the henhouse. If he stays working for me, maybe he'll learn a thing or two about being a good cowboy instead of a bully."

At that moment, Bo could see the shine of understanding in Leonard's eyes. *The boy probably didn't think anyone understood what he was feeling.* He hoped that Leonard could see that he was trying to help him navigate his way through what would be, in retrospect one day, a minor problem. "Now, you reckon you're done ruminating, or do I need to find another ranch hand?"

Leonard beamed from ear to ear. "Yes sir," he said, nodding his head. "Um, no sir," he said, shaking his head. Then he shook his head crazily.

Bo laughed.

Leonard then turned toward the house and shouted to his mother, "Mom, I'm going to work!"

Bo suspected she'd heard the whole thing. Most women had bionic hearing, after all. He could hear the plates clanging and glasses ringing through the open kitchen window as she and Jenny fussed in the kitchen.

"Change your shoes, son!" was her shout back.

Leonard ran to the back porch where he kept an old, dirty pair of tennis shoes, perfectly suited for stomping around in horse stalls. He plopped down on the bench to change shoes. When he looked up, he saw Bo waiting.

Bo said, "Well, are you going to poke around here all morning, or do you want a ride?"

Leonard freaked out. "Really?"

"It would be a lot faster than walking, and you're late for work already," Bo said, grinning.

Leonard opted for bare feet temporarily, grabbing up his old shoes, tying the laces together, and flinging them over his shoulder. He leaped from the back porch and shouted, "Bye, Mom!" as he ran through the grass, toes digging in all the way to the fence. He spread the lower two sections of barbed wire and slid through one leg at a time. Bo leaned over in the saddle and extended his arm, locking his hand with Leonard's and pulling him up. The leather creaked as it stretched—an intoxicating sound to this old rancher. And for Leonard, Bo knew this was probably the first time he'd heard that sound and would probably remember it for the rest of his life—connected to the joy and freedom in this day.

———•———

Try as she might, her voice failed her, cracking as she tried unsuccessfully to holler out a goodbye. Surprised at the intensity of her emotion, Lynette struggled to compose herself. She'd witnessed the raw joy in her son's movements and words as he jumped onto Whisky's back. She knew, at that moment, Leonard had crossed a threshold that would usher him into manhood. The realization was overpowering to her. This little moment was one of the most important of his young life, one that a boy could only experience with the guidance of a man. Serendipity had placed Bo Kelso in that position for Leonard, on behalf of Leonard's late father Levi.

She covered her face with a dishtowel, muffling her happy sobbing, as she internalized the vision of her son on that horse. Not wanting to miss a minute, she moved as close as she could to the kitchen window, then the back screen door, and eventually onto the back porch. She sat on the bench and watched Whisky's long tail swishing back and forth, until the image faded into a memory.

"Oh, Levi, did you see that?" Lynette wiped away more tears from her cheek. "That boy is growing up so fast. Thank God for this moment, and thank you for giving him to me." She whispered a short prayer and lingered a few minutes more to ensure she hadn't missed an extra second of the cowboy, her son, and that beautiful horse.

Just then, Jenny emerged from the house holding a large kitchen towel. When she observed her beloved caretaker sitting on the bench and crying, she placed both her hands on her hips and asked, "What happened? Did that man say something to make you cry?"

"No dear, I'm just happy, that's all."

"But you're crying."

"Yes, I am crying tears of joy. I am crying because I'm happy. When you're real happy, the kind of happy I am right now, you cry," Lynette said and then stood from the bench. Placing her arm around the young girl, they returned to the kitchen.

"Men!" Jenny said, causing Lynette to howl in hearty laughter.

# 34

"Well, ain't that a sight to see," Matt said, scratching his sweat-soaked head, looking off into the pasture.

Kevin stopped with wheelbarrow still in hand, on his way back from the compost heap, and took a look himself. He saw the outline of a horse and a rider emerging just a short distance away. "So what? It's just Mr. Kelso," Kevin said.

"Looks like Old Man Kelso found himself a pet monkey."

*Matt must be hittin' those beers again,* Kevin thought, but then he put two and two together. Leonard was also riding on the back of Whisky.

Matt continued his rude comedy: "He must've ridden too close to the tree line, and one fell out of the oak trees onto Whisky's back."

"That's it!"

Kevin dropped the wheelbarrow hard, causing the pitchfork and shovel to roll out onto the ground. The sound startled Matt, who turned to his left, just in time to see Kevin running full stride at him. Matt did not even have time to turn his feet, as he was still oriented toward the pasture, holding a feed bucket in each hand. Kevin collided with him at a full run. He leapt into the air like a tiger on the hunt and wrapped his arms around Matt's neck, striking him off balance.

Matt dropped the feed buckets as he flipped over to his right side, rolling two full turns before coming to a stop. Kevin wrapped his legs around Matt's waist, and with both hands firmly locked around his neck, he started to squeeze like an anaconda. Matt tried to pull Kevin's hands apart from around his neck, to no avail. Kevin's years of swimming had given him great strength in his arms, maybe the strength of two twelve-year-olds, and that was as good as one twenty-four-year-old man in Kevin's mind. He had just flat out had enough.

Matt desperately tried to free his neck from the grip of Kevin's arms. When that did not work, he struggled and eventually got to his feet. He swung his fists wildly, attempting to hit Kevin's head, which was tucked in tight to Matt's neck. Kevin could feel Matt's razor stubble against his own cheek as Matt swung and punched wildly in an attempt to free himself.

"Take it back!" Kevin screamed. "You take it back right now!"

Matt could not have answered even if he wanted to. He was losing air, and the more he struggled, the weaker his punches became. Matt needed saving, in more ways than one.

———•———

Bo could not believe what he was seeing. At the same time, he knew it was as real as the dust flying and arms flailing. This was no game. As he made to put his heels to Whisky and get to the barn pronto, he felt Leonard dismounting without warning. Casting his shoes from around his shoulders onto the grass, Leonard hit the ground in forward progress, legs a blur of motion, bare feet kicking up dirt. Whisky startled at this surprise move, so much so that he failed for a moment to obey rein and heel commands from Bo. Struggling to turn Whisky and bring him under control, Bo watched as Leonard had already closed the gap between them and Matt with Kevin affixed firmly to his neck.

Whether or not Matt could see Leonard coming, Bo didn't know, but the boy launched his body full force into Matt's chest and knocked him back on to the ground.

"Let go of my friend!" Leonard yelled at the top of his lungs as he, too, clamored over Matt.

Kevin still had a hold of Matt's neck, and his legs were

wrapped tightly around Matt's waist. Just then, Bo saw Clint sprinting from the end of the barn and toward the cloud of dust that was now three boys flopping around in the dirt.

Bo stopped Whisky a few feet away from Leonard's shoulder and Whisky's head dropped down and almost touched Matt's cowboy boots. Matt stopped struggling and started lightly tapping on Kevin's arm. His body was positioned on top of Kevin's like two turtles struggling to right themselves after falling off a ledge. Matt had given in; he was defeated. The combined effort of the two boys protecting each other was too much for him. Besides, Bo was there now. The fight would have to stop.

"You take it back, Matt!" Kevin shouted one last time.

Matt nodded his head in an attempt to speak.

"Loosen up on him a little, boy. He can't talk," Bo said.

As Kevin did this, Matt replied, "Okay, I didn't mean it, I take it back. Are you happy now?"

Kevin released his grip and jumped to his feet, satisfied that he was the victor.

Matt sat up but did not get on his feet. Leonard stood with both of his fists clenched, watching to make sure Matt was not going to retaliate.

"That's enough, all of you." Bo's voice was commanding and firm. It was all that was needed. Everyone, except for Whisky, stopped. The horse took a step forward and brushed his snout up on the side of Matt's face, curious at the spectacle of him sitting on the ground and struggling to catch his breath.

"He started this whole thing; he jumped on me from behind and started choking me for no reason."

"I had a reason, Mr. Kelso."

"I don't care what your reasons were. If you boys want to fight each other, that's fine, but you do it somewhere else," Bo said. "You'll spook the horses."

Clint had stopped just short of the fighting circle and now took a couple steps closer. "Well, I can see that the gang's all here now. Stop wasting your time playing in the dirt and use that energy to clean the stalls. You've entertained the livestock long enough."

Clint walked past the tangle of youths and glanced up at Bo with a smile so wide Bo thought he would break into hysterics. But in seconds, he was wearing that same smile. The two men were aware of the significance of this moment, these past few days, remembering similar moments from their childhood, when they became men from boys. And best of all, they knew they'd played a big role in setting this feat in motion. Bo knew Clint felt similarly, the satisfaction filling up as many empty spaces as possible in their hearts.

———•———

An unspoken but workable relationship was forged between the three young men. They each worked their ends of the barn cleaning stalls and feeding horses. Matt got used to feeding the goats and stopped complaining. He stopped pushing Kevin's buttons. He tolerated Leonard without harm. The three to four hours of work each morning passed quickly and without incident. Clint occasionally worked the weekends alone, giving the other three some slack in their ropes to pursue other passions.

Matt's questionable habits of overindulgence and tardiness continued, but were improving slowly. Bo kept him on. Even an ugly cow needed a herd to graze with.

# 35

The last days of summer vacation were closing in on the lives of Kevin and Leonard. They felt each tick of the second hand as it hastily chiseled away at their freedom with each passing of its hand across the faces of the watches they each now wore. These new wristwatches were another reminder that life was changing and they were becoming young men with responsibilities. There were appointments to keep, deadlines that must be met, schedules. As the summer began to melt into a new school year and a new season, the time they spent together now was like gold. They instinctively understood the power of the second hand. Even though they still had a little more than three weeks before school started up again, the dread of boarding the school bus each day and being caged up in a room, while the sun shined and the fish jumped, weighed heavily upon their thoughts. One more day of carrying a tackle box instead of a book bag would enable them to store one more memory in their young minds to cherish for a lifetime.

This Saturday was bright as always, but the air was unseasonably cool, the temperature hovering around seventy-eight degrees. Planning a full day of fishing at the sand mine, Kevin and Leonard decided to swing by the barn first to see if Bo wanted to go with them. If not, they would happily walk the three-mile trail through the forest and pastures to fish on the abandoned beach together.

Before they'd made it off of Kevin's back porch, they ran into his father, who was sitting on the stoop, lacing up his work boots. He didn't usually work on Saturdays, but today was an exception. "Are you sure you boys can carry that icebox all the way to the back of the ranch?" Allen asked, looking at the cooler the boys had dropped at his side. "I can take you to the back fence on the other side of Clear Creek on my way in this morning, if you'd like. It would cut down the walk by a good two miles or so."

"That's okay, Dad. We're going to go by the barn on our way and see if Mr. Kelso wants to go with us for a little while. If he does, he will take us there," Kevin explained as he closed the lid on a thirty-two-quart Igloo cooler.

Allen reopened it. Inside there was enough food to feed a whole troop of hungry Boy Scouts. They had rescued every Tupperware container full of leftovers that was soon destined for the compost heap or the dog bowl. These leftovers were jammed randomly into the cooler along with Dr. Pepper bottles and a half jug of sweet tea.

"Is this your mama's chicken gumbo that we had last night?" Allen asked as he rummaged around inside the cooler.

"Not all of it, Dad," Kevin explained.

"Well, it sure does look like a whole lot of it, and I like your mama's chicken gumbo."

"It's okay, Dad. Mom told me to take all I wanted because she's cooking a fresh pot of shrimp gumbo tonight."

"Well, in that case, I can't see any reason why I should fight you boys for it. I'll see you when I get home this afternoon. Y'all have a good time and stay out of trouble." He punctuated that with a slap of his hands on his thighs. He then stood up and made his way in the early morning light to his truck.

Kevin and Leonard tucked their fishing rods under their arms and their tackle boxes in one hand, and carried the big cooler between them. They entered the pasture through the barbed wire fence as always, bringing their supplies with them.

It didn't take them long to realize they were overloaded with far too much equipment. When they stopped by the barn, Leonard suggested they should borrow a wheelbarrow to put all the items in and return it when they came back. Grateful for the hope of some relief from the weight, Kevin agreed wholeheartedly. When they arrived at the barn, they saw Clint, alone with his small transistor radio, which he hung on a nail on the wall. These were the sounds of "pure country gold," Clint had told them when they'd first started working here. Someone was singing a cowboy song, which neither of the boys could identify.

————•————

Clint had already finished the feeding and upkeep on the one side of the barn as the horses on the other side waited their turns. Upon seeing the two boys enter the other end of the barn, the horses started to whinny in their direction, knowing that they would soon be fed now that the reinforcements had arrived.

"Who is that?" Leonard asked, referring to the singer on the radio.

"Well, if you were truly a cowboy, you would know who that was singing," Clint replied with a gentle smile, taking in the sight of these two spindly boys struggling to carry all of their fishing equipment and an enormous cooler. "Looks like the two of you need a wheelbarrow."

"Yes. We'll bring it back when were done. We are going to the old sand mine and spend the whole day fishing. It's a perfect day for it," Leonard said.

"We were wondering if Mr. Kelso would like to go with us this morning," Kevin said.

"Well, you're running a little late. Mr. Kelso and Whisky headed out before the sun was even up. Just so you know, boys . . . today is the anniversary of his wife's passing. I'm sure he's going up to spend time at the graveyard. You'll be passing right by him, so you can invite him fishing when you see him." Clint leaned into his office door. "Here, you better take this with you." He emerged from his office holding a rod and reel that they'd bought a few days ago as a belated gift to Bo, a trophy for the enormous bass he'd let go. Clint smiled as the boys added it to the growing pile of gear.

They retrieved a wheelbarrow and put the icebox and both tackle boxes in it. They tucked the rods in with the tips facing to the front, thanking Clint before running toward the bridge.

Clint touched the brim of his hat and grinned as the bobbers bounced up and down with every bump of the wheelbarrow. He watched the boys making their hasty way down the dirt road to the bridge. He felt like he was with them in spirit. He shouted, "Good luck!" just before they rounded the corner. Kevin turned and waved back in Clint's direction as Leonard soldiered forward with the wheelbarrow.

---

The two of them made good time, taking turns with the wheelbarrow through the pastures along the rim of Clear Creek. The dew on the grass soaked their tennis shoes and made the wheel of the wheelbarrow glisten a shimmering black, flinging droplets of water all along the bottom.

Upon clearing the thicket and a corner of tall pines and magnificent oaks, they came upon a picnic area covered in buttercups and bluebonnets. The colors stretched from the edge of the thicket, far across to the graveyard, and all the way down to Clear Creek.

Off to their left, not more than a stone's throw short of the graveyard fence, they saw Whisky. He stood there alone, saddled, his bridle reins hanging down into the tall grass and the wildflowers, most of which were knee-high on the boys. Though the horse seemed calm enough, the boys sensed something was up.

Without a word of discussion, they dropped everything and ran to Whisky. Kevin got there first, and that's when he saw Bo, stretched out on the grass. His face looked pained, and he was holding his chest. Seconds later, Leonard stopped short at Kevin's side.

"Hello, boys," Bo said as he gasped for breath.

"Did you fall off your horse?" Kevin asked.

"Do you need us to get help?" Leonard asked.

"What happened, Mr. Kelso?"

"Are you hurt?"

The questions came faster than Bo would ever be able to answer them, and their voices began to run together. "You could say I fell off my horse," he replied, then changed the subject. "I see you boys are on your way to go fishing."

Their friend was in obvious discomfort, his face a gray color, his lips slightly blue. He did not look good. Kevin turned to Leonard and told him to run fast and get some help. Something was wrong. Leonard turned to start a fast trek back to Clint, when Bo stopped him, summoned him back.

"Hold up, boy. I'm going to be fine. You just come back here for a minute because I have something I need to tell you, but I need to tell you together."

Kevin and Leonard were confused and a little scared. It was obvious to them that Bo needed help, but they dared not disobey their mentor and friend.

Still, they begged permission. "Mr. Kelso, you look like you need some help," Leonard said. "Let me take Whisky and ride back to the barn and tell Clint."

"No, boy. I need the two of you to stay with me because you must do something for me," Bo said in a weary voice. "Besides, Whisky won't leave me here. He probably thinks it's his fault I fell off him. Fact is, boys, I'm going to die this time. I can feel it. This ain't the first time I have had one of these spells, but this time, I am ready to go. And there's no place I'd rather do that than here," he said, pulling one of his legs up in an attempt to ease his pain.

"Then we need to go get help for you right away!" Leonard's pitch rose as he fought back the urge to cry, to yell, to disobey, to run for help.

"I appreciate that, son, but there is nothing you can do to stop what is going to happen. It's extremely important to me that the two of you hear what I have to say, and then I'll let you go get help, okay?" Bo scanned their frightened eyes and held their hands as they kneeled next to him in an attempt to calm them down. "I have watched you boys grow up together over the short summer that we shared. You have learned so much, and I am so impressed with the two of you. You are from fine stock and that in itself is truly a blessing. I'm sorry I don't have the time to teach you boys more about being a cowboy. But I'm going to tell you a story that I hope you understand, and then I'm going to ask you to do something for me."

Bo struggled with his words. He directed the boys to remove his saddlebags from Whisky and place them under his head so he could see the waters of Clear Creek.

"Be careful now, boy, there's a loaded pistol in that saddle bag. You just leave it where it is," Bo warned as Kevin retrieved the saddlebag.

Whisky gently nuzzled the side of Bo's face, and he in turn reached up and rubbed his loyal steed from ears to jawbone, trying to reassure the horse as much as the boys.

"Boys, one of the true facts of life is we only have to do two things with it: we have to believe in something in order to live our lives, and we have to die, a price we pay for the joy of living. Everything else in between is what we do to supplement our souls while we're living. I have lived a wonderful life, and I've believed in things that kept me alive and gave me pleasure. I have done good things, and I have done some things I'm not proud of. Along the way, I have paid for and corrected those mistakes, save one."

Kevin and Leonard said not a word, but listened with grave faces.

"Now you boys just listen to what I have to tell you. I have an appointment to keep, and what you do with what I tell you has a great bearing on that meeting. Even if you don't do what I ask of you, just you listening will do me a world of good. You boys aren't Catholic, are you?" he asked in a joking manner.

"No sir!" the boys said in unison, "we're Baptist." The joke went sailing over their heads into the pasture yonder.

Even in his most dire hour, Bo found a way to diffuse the finality of the moment. He asked them to remove a diary from the saddlebag. As Kevin pulled the diary from it, a small paper bag with a half-sliced apple fell to the ground—Whisky's treat. Then Bo began to narrate the story of the tractor he'd bought in 1942.

From his father and grandfather, he had learned of prejudice. His family had been cruel to the sharecroppers who walked many miles to provide backbreaking labor at the ranch in return for meager pennies in wages. As Bo grew, so did his discomfort with these injustices. He swore to himself that when he took over the farm, he would not be like them. Things would be different.

There was a day when Bo had to leave town to sell cattle at an auction in San Antonio. The majority of the ranch hands were gone because most of the livestock had already been shipped off to San Antonio. Only a few hands were left to tend to the remaining livestock. The only black hand at the time was a man he had recently hired, a strong, twenty-year-old black man with eyes of blue. He had only been working on the ranch for a few days and kept to himself mostly. He was not overly welcomed by the rest of the crew.

That weekend in July 1942, the weather forecast was steady rain from Friday morning to Monday afternoon. Before Bo left for San Antonio, he parked his new tractor under a small pole barn that held several wagons and two other tractors. The pole barn had a tin roof that would shelter the equipment from the weather. After returning home once the storms had passed, the pole barn stood, but the tractor was gone. And there was only one man to blame, in Bo's opinion.

In 1983, a fierce storm rose up from the Gulf of Mexico and marched across the farmlands, drenching it with enormous amounts of rain. The rain overflowed the banks of Clear Creek. The creek usually was no more than two feet deep, maybe ten feet wide. The edges of the creek had a steep grade that dropped off more than twenty-five feet to the bottom. Still, during this storm, the creek overflowed its banks, turning the meandering waterway into a torrent, wider than one hundred yards and as deep as fifty feet in some places. The swelling waters twisted and turned as it washed away the banks and cut into the land. It also cut into a small pond that was no more than fifty yards from the pole barn. The old pole barn, now just a shelter for the cattle to escape the blistering rays of the summer Texas sun, fell over in submission to the gale-force winds. It was reduced to a pile of twisted tin and partially broken, leaning creosote posts.

That pond had been dug so the cattle could drink without venturing down the treacherous slopes of Clear Creek in order to quench their thirst. When the storm passed and the water level started to fall, it cut through the property and crossed the small pond. The incredible flow of water cut a ravine deep enough to connect the small pond to Clear Creek and drained the pond. The pond, now void of water, exposed a Farmall tractor sitting right in the middle of it. It had been there more than forty-two years, submerged and holding on to the truth.

Bo had then pondered the evidence, figuring he had not applied the brake after parking it that summer in 1942. It must have rolled backward into the pond some time during that storm. All the heavy rain that weekend had washed away any tracks or signs that would reveal his mistake. As he had spent four decades assuming the rain had washed away tracks of the thief, the rain had actually washed away the traces of his own forgetfulness.

"I swore up and down that Mr. Elijah Waters stole that tractor," Bo gasped as sorrowful tears filled his eyes. "I had the law arrest him. They were cruel and beat him in order to make him confess, but he never did. They beat that man so severely that it opened a gash as wide as my thumb on the left side of his head. They had him handcuffed and shackled to a heavy steel chair. The deputies left him like that for almost two days. I went to the sheriff's office on the third day to check and see if they found my tractor. One of the deputies looked up at me and said, 'He's one stubborn nigger. We've tried everything short of cutting his throat, but nothing seems to work.'

"The deputy then led me into the room, flipping on a single overhead bulb to illuminate where Elijah had been for two days, chained to a chair. His pants were soiled, and the room smelled worse than a pigsty. They had shoved him into the far corner of the cinderblock room face down on the floor with the chair legs sticking up in the air. He was lying there unconscious, chained to a chair in the darkness.

"That deputy hollered, 'Rise and shine, boy. It's time to go at it again.' When Elijah did not respond, the lawman grabbed the chair and dragged it across the room, scraping Elijah's face on the concrete. The cuts on his face that had finally dried shut now tore open again, and fresh blood oozed from his face. Then another deputy came into the room, and they sat the chair up on its legs. Elijah's limp body slumped over; his chin touched his knees.

"They dragged a small, square table with steel legs over in front of him, and one of the deputies sat on top of it, crossed one leg over the other and his hands over his crossed knees. The ten-by-ten block room with no windows and only one way in and out was crowded with the four of us, and the stench invaded our nostrils. The first deputy reached up and grabbed Elijah's hair, then pulled him up in the chair to reveal the crusted dried blood from his forehead down to his T-shirt.

"Boys, Elijah had endured cruelty that I set into motion. I left the room, knowing that they'd started in on him again. As I walked down the hallway to the front office, I could hear them pounding their fists on him."

Bo started to cough violently, doubling over in pain. He drew up his knees and then relaxed back onto the saddle bag. However, the pain he was feeling was not as much from his chest as it was from his memories. "I didn't feel the impact of those thuds for more than forty-two years. I didn't see the blood on his face or feel the pain he endured . . . because I was a heartless bastard. When I found that tractor at the bottom of the cattle tank, all the emotions I should've felt years ago caught up with me in a flash.

"All I'd cared about was that damn tractor. A pile of metal perched on top of rubber tires. I valued that over the flesh and soul of an innocent man." Bo choked, tears drizzling down the sides of his face like rain—like the rain that had washed away the tractor and the rain that had allowed it to resurface those so many years ago.

"The entire colored community tried to convince me otherwise about Elijah, but I would hear none of it. I had thoroughly convinced myself that he'd done it. My reasoning? Because he hadn't shown up for work when I got back from San Antonio. Well, when they kicked down the door to his house in Clover Town, he was holding his newborn daughter in his arms. He had been up for thirty-six hours straight delivering her. His family told me the baby'd almost died during the delivery. That's why he hadn't shown up for work. But I didn't care. I carried the sins of my fathers with me, convinced that Elijah had stolen that tractor, and he did it because he was black and poor. No other reason than that."

Bo paused to reach out for a bundle of wildflowers that he'd dropped during his fall to the ground. They were a mixture of blue, red, and yellow, and buttercups, which he'd bound together with a hair ribbon from Mary Beth's vanity. He'd picked them on his way to the graveyard he never reached.

"It took every dime his friends and family had to hire a good white lawyer and keep him out of jail. Thank God, there wasn't enough evidence to convict him. They found him not guilty.

After the trial, he joined the Navy. I never saw him or his family again after that. I'd spent forty-two years hating a man because of what I foolishly thought he did, because he was colored and poor. The prejudice poked through my skin like a thorn on a briar, and I used it to harm another. I had become what I swore I would never be. When I saw that tractor sitting at the bottom of the tank, I knew what I was and how sorry a man I really had been all these years.

"When I saw the tractor that morning, I was determined to drag it out of there myself. I took a chain from the back of my truck, crawled out onto the lake bed on my hands and knees on account of the mud being so thick. My boots got stuck my first two steps and came off. Once I secured the chain to the front axle of the rusted-out old tractor, I pulled myself back up to the bank one hand over the other, grasping the chain for dear life. I lay on my back covered in mud, gasping for breath. My heart was pounding like a hammer on an anvil, so badly that I thought my chest would explode and my heart would fall back into the tank. But I was so ashamed of myself that I refused to die right there and be caught red-handed with the evidence of my prejudiced ways.

"The mud was so thick on my hands and clothes—thick as the shame I felt in my heart now that I knew the truth. It covered my body and crippled me to the point where I could not use my hands in order to get my keys out of my pocket. I had to rinse myself off in the creek bed in order to get them out. I sat there on the bank of the creek, crying as I felt the mud, still on my face, dry and tighten my skin. I still taste the mixture of mud and tears in my mouth every time I think about that morning.

"I returned later that afternoon, after I caught my breath, and I used the big tractor from the hay barn to drag the old Farmall out of the tank bed. The wheels were rusted solid and gouged ruts into the road and pasture all the way to the ravine where I hid it yonder." Bo raised his arm and pointed to the edge of the thicket. There was a deep ravine where they'd been dumping old parts and implements for as far back as the Civil War.

"The scars that tractor made on the land, when I dragged it, healed up after a few weeks worth of rain and the livestock traipsing across the road, but my scars—they never healed. I covered it up with the tin roof from the shelter that fell down in a pitiful attempt to hide my shame.

"The following day, after tossing and turning all night, I vowed to track down Elijah and make a grand apology to him and his family, and that's when I learned something else." Bo closed his eyes and was still, but only momentarily. He abruptly began to shake, the tears breaking the boundaries of his eyelids and lashes. "I am a coward; I haven't yet been able to bring myself to do it."

Kevin turned and looked at Leonard, who was crying without restraint. He realized they'd just heard a confession, and even at their young age, they had been charged with a great task.

Bo's skin was now an ash gray and his lips much bluer. This time Leonard did not ask as he turned and sped back to the barn.

Bo handed the small, black journal to Kevin, explaining that everything he needed to know in order to find Elijah Waters was in the book. He assured Kevin that his sons in Houston would provide them with the money necessary to find Elijah. He said that tucked within those pages were also notes for his sons and his grandchildren, which he had written months ago after his first heart attack. Therein, he had given instructions for his sons to help Kevin and Leonard find Elijah, in the event that he died before he got the chance to do it himself. He wrote that he had chosen the boys to be his messengers because he looked upon them as being flawless and genuinely without prejudice.

"Now, you take this book and give it to my son, and he will help you find Elijah. When you meet, you will know it's him because his eyes are as blue as the skies above us and the waters of the deepest lake. He has the eyes of an honest man. Tell him how sorry I am for what I've done to him, and be sure you look into his blue eyes when you deliver that message."

Whisky's muzzle was never more than a few inches away from Bo during this conversation, as if sensing his friend was in peril and needed his support. Kevin also sat at Bo's side, long enough to watch the color of his skin fade to a pale white. He asked him repeatedly if he was okay, if there was something he could do to ease his pain, but Bo only shook his head slightly. His breath became shallower, until it eventually faded into nothing. Kevin leaned over and placed his ear to Bo's mouth and nose. He then put his fingers to Bo's neck. He could not find a pulse or breath going in or out.

Everything was so peaceful there by the gravesite. Barely a sound could be heard, save for the song of a mockingbird as it perched on a limb of a dogwood tree. *Nothing more can be done now*, Kevin thought. *It's what Mr. Kelso wanted.* He waited for Leonard and wondered why he hadn't yet shed a tear of his own.

Kevin started questioning his emotions. Why hadn't he cried yet, like Leonard? Why was he so calm during a situation that most people, young or adult, would panic over? He reasoned that perhaps it was because he knew it was what Mr. Kelso wanted and that the old man found comfort in that decision. Even if he could have saved Mr. Kelso, he doubted he could have overcome his resolve. This was Mr. Kelso's choice to make, and this was the place he wanted to be when his time came.

Kevin retrieved a beach towel from the wheelbarrow and covered covered Bo's face and upper torso with it. He then picked up the paper bag, removed the apple slice, and held it in his hand palm up for Whisky, who sniffed it, pulled it into his lips, then held it for a few seconds without chewing. For the first time since the boys had gotten there, Whisky turned away from his cowboy and finished eating.

Leonard was the first to return, well ahead of the others that had to take the long way around the creek by truck in order to reach the wildflower patch. He was short of breath when he fell to his knees next to Bo. He looked at Kevin, who held his gaze as he slowly shook his head back and forth.

Leonard whispered, "Are you sure?"

"Yes, I am sure. When will help be here?"

"Clint called for an ambulance and he also called Mr. Kelso's sons, Clay and Jeb. He is behind me in the truck. He should be here in a few minutes."

Leonard lifted the towel just high enough to look at Bo's face, and Kevin looked too; it was even whiter now than when Kevin had first placed the towel over it. Neither of the boys had ever seen a dead person before and was not sure how to react. As Leonard replaced the towel, Kevin noticed a small drop of water fall from the sky, making a perfect circle on the fabric, then another and another. The raindrops fell into a tight group and faded into one expanding spot. Kevin's stare fixed on the gathering droplets, mesmerized at the thought of rain falling on one concentrated area.

"How could it be raining in just one place and not on me. I don't feel the rain on my neck," Kevin said, swiping at his neck, staring at the spot. Then he knew. Leonard's composure had exploded, and he now sobbed loudly, sorrowful and without shame. The raindrops that Kevin had witness had come from his best friend's heart.

Within a few minutes, the peaceful field was filled with people and trucks. The ambulance drivers loaded Bo onto a stretcher and strapped him down. The EMTs removed a clean white sheet from a shiny metal cabinet in the van. Kevin noticed the smell of fresh linen, which was so strong that it overpowered the natural floral fragrance as they snapped the sheet open and placed it over the body, on top of the beach towel. The folded lines of the sheet were sharp and maintained their square shape in a symmetrical form from Bo Kelso's head to his boots.

The sons arrived—Jeb first, then Clay a short time later.

Soon the tears were dropping like rain again, wetting the earth that Bo so loved.

Clint removed his hat as he struggled to one knee in order to lean down close to his friend's ear. He whispered, "Nutmeg, Bo. It was nutmeg that made her coffee taste so good. I would have told you sooner, but I'd made Mary Beth a promise. I guess it doesn't matter so much now, but at the time, that secret helped lure you out of the house. But of course you know that now, don't you, old man?"

Clint returned the sheet to cover Bo's face. He then picked up Whisky's reins, quietly leading the horse away.

"He is with her now. He will be fine," Clint whispered in a cracking voice to Clay and Jeb as he walked past them. He replaced the hat on his head, and he did not cry.

Clay rode in the ambulance with his father, and Jeb stayed behind to handle immediate concerns at the ranch.

"Come on, Kevin, Clint is going to give us a ride back to our houses in his truck," Leonard said.

"That's okay. I'll help you load the stuff up in the truck, but I'm going to walk home," Kevin said. He bent down and picked up the bundle of flowers that Bo had picked for Mary Beth's grave.

Jeb followed behind Kevin as he made his way to the graveyard. He trailed back just far enough to allow Kevin some privacy as he stepped through the iron gates and walked up to Mary Beth's gravestone. He bent down at the waist and placed the flowers on top of her headstone. The tears finally came for Kevin. Without a word, Jeb sat down on the concrete bench just outside of the archway and patiently waited for Kevin to have this moment.

"I'll give you a ride home, if you'd like," Jeb said as he stood and greeted Kevin just outside the gate.

"That's okay. It's not too far to my house, and I'd rather walk."

Jeb held out Bo's journal to Kevin. He said, "My brother and

I have been reading this since we got here, and it seems like my father has one last task to complete. The only problem is, now he'll need you and Leonard to do it for him."

"I know. He told us all about it before he died. I'm not sure if I can do what he wants me to do," Kevin said as he hung his head down and stared at the sea of wildflowers at his feet.

Jeb let a second pass and then said, "Well, one thing I feel certain is that you are indeed the man for the job. My daddy wouldn't have said so if it weren't true. If you'll allow me to take you home, I could speak to your parents about it . . . is that okay with you?"

Kevin looked up into Jeb's eyes and nodded.

# 36

"This place reminds me of home—don't you think so, Kevin?" Leonard's nose was smooshed into the window of the passenger plane as he gazed at the land below him. The plane slowly banked to the left and turned on its final approach into the small airport of New Bern, North Carolina. Kevin leaned across Leonard's shoulder to get a better view as the plane leveled its wings over the Neuse River. He could see the Neuse and the Trent rivers as they joined and wrapped their waters around the small city at its banks. New Bern was bigger than their little town in Texas.

"Yeah, it does, but the rivers are a lot bigger," Kevin remarked, and Leonard nodded his head in agreement.

Clay, who had been sitting in the seat across the aisle, gestured to them and turned their attention to the view from his side of the airplane. From the edge of the water to the horizon was nothing but trees. Majestic pines rose more than a hundred feet into the air and oaks with leaves as broad as the palm of your hand waved at them. Clay was happy to see that this small waterfront town, even though larger than their own, had a harmony and balance of the land and water.

"Oh boy, this is nothing like I thought it would be," Leonard said to Clay.

"And what did you think it would be, Leonard?"

"I thought it would look like New York City, with one tall building after another."

A few minutes later, they were on the ground. There were no automated walkways, elevators, or stairs. They simply disembarked via a set of aluminum steps that were pushed up against the open door of the small airplane. They then walked across an exposed area of the tarmac to the terminal. It too was small. A simple metal building housed the departing and arriving passengers. The baggage was handled in the same manner: a flatbed truck removed the baggage from the belly of the airplane and deposited it at the edge of the building where the passengers retrieved it. This was very different from the way passengers and baggage were handled at the comparatively massive Houston International Airport.

When they entered the small terminal, bags in hand, Mr. Waters's granddaughter Lee Ann met them. Lee Ann was the first person Clay had gotten in touch with after he spoke to Pastor Clover at the Clover Town Pentecostal Church.

Pastor Clover told Clay that she had been investigating her family's history for a paper she was writing in college. She spent several weeks researching her family's background and speaking to her grandfather about his childhood growing up in the deep south. That is when he told her of the little church he'd attended in Texas. It was the church where he and her grandmother had been married. He described in detail the farmland and pastures that stretched as far as the eye could see and how the white-faced cattle dotted the fields, enjoying the bounty of their land. He spoke of Clear Creek cutting through the property, dividing it like a painter's brush saturated in clear blue, shimmering color.

It was at that creek where he would catch the catfish that first his mother and then his young wife would fry up for dinner. It was also the creek where he was baptized. He recounted to Lee Ann how young he had been at the time, standing no higher than the preacher's waist, wearing only his undershorts and his father's cleanest white T-shirt, which covered him all the way down to his knees. His family and friends stood on the steep banks of Clear Creek, dressed in white shirts or draped in white sheets fashioned around their bodies; the women's heads were wrapped in white cloth. The day had been a typical July scorcher as he stepped into the sandy bottom of the creek and felt the soothing coolness of the water touching his skin. With a backward dip by the strong arms of Pastor Clover, he was proclaimed free of sin and a true child of God.

The waters of Clear Creek provided him with his first feeling of accomplishment in being able to provide a meal for his family, whether it be catfish or snapping turtle. It was also the place where he gave his first flower, kiss, and ultimately, his heart forever to the girl he loved when he proposed to Lee Ann's grandmother. He'd gotten on one knee and took her hand. One foot slipped into the creek and the other knee was firmly planted in the sand as he looked up at her standing above him on the bank and pledged his love eternal.

The creek was also where he had first experienced the sting of racial insult. Horrible words were hurled at him and his friends from the ranch hands atop their horses as they warned them not to cross the creek or bother the cattle. It was the first time a white man had ever called him a nigger, and he knew even at such a young age that it was venom, spoken in such a manner to convey hatred. And so with that memory, the waters of Clear Creek were also a boundary that divided him from what he always thought of as another man's land—in more ways than one.

These stories shared with Lee Ann by her grandfather Elijah sparked her interest, and she looked forward to the next time together on the porch, hearing the next story spoken in his low, tender voice. His stories were vivid, told with clarity and passion, as they looked beyond the backyard of his home in James City to the waters of the Neuse River and the buildings of downtown New Bern.

While his stories of youth were impactful, his stories of war were even more impressive.

He had served as a cook in the Navy during World War II and retired as a first class petty officer after twenty-one years. His last duty station was a small Coast Guard station in Morehead City, North Carolina. He told his daughter that this was his calling—because he loved the water so much, he always wanted to look out his window and see it.

<hr />

"Well, this is it," Lee Ann said as she pulled up into the long driveway to her grandfather's house. The Neuse River stretched out behind it like a carpet of blue flowers waving in the evening breeze. The breeze was lightly blowing through the leaves of the pecan trees that lined the drive. Several squirrels scattered from the ground to the safety of the towering trees as Lee Ann drove up the drive to the house.

"That's my grandma. She has to fight the squirrels every year in order to gather up enough pecans for her pies." She stuck her arm out the window and returned the wave from her grandmother who was walking through the yard with a full tray of drinks and cookies.

"She's been baking all day; wait until you taste her pecan cookies, but don't eat too many," Lee Ann warned in a friendly tone. "You will have to save room for dinner. She is the best cook ever. When I'm home from school, I stay in that small guesthouse. You are going to love it too. The breeze blowing in off the Neuse River is so cool here at night, you don't even need the air conditioning."

The car came to a stop between the main house and the small thirty-by-thirty guesthouse. It had a screened in porch on the front that provided protection from the bugs and added to the charm of the building, which was painted the same color as the main house. The grounds and buildings were clean and neatly maintained. It reminded Kevin of the fine homes in his mother's *Southern Living* magazines. Mrs. Waters approached the four as they got out of the car and smiled from ear to ear with a genuine smile that assured them they were most welcome here.

"Give me a hand, Lee Ann," she said as she held out the

tray. Lee Ann took it and introduced Kevin, Clay, and Leonard. "We are so glad to see you; I hope your trip was a good one. We have the guesthouse all ready for you. Come on and let's put your things away while Lee Ann puts the tray on the back porch."

Kevin, Clay, and Leonard felt right at home. It was as if they had only walked across the street to a friend's house. The only difference was the water.

"What a spectacular view you have," Clay said appreciatively as he stopped to take in the beauty of the Neuse River from the edge of the porch. The thick, freshly cut St. Augustine grass was a flawless green, without a single weed to mar it. An uninterrupted perfect patch of grass stretched over fifty yards to the water's edge, where it abruptly ended at a sandy beach, which then intermingled with the gentle waves of the Neuse.

"I am glad you like it. We planted the St. Augustine grass because it reminds us of our first home in Texas," Mrs. Waters told them. "I am sure Clover Town has changed a lot since we left there in 1942. Now come on inside. We need to hide you three before Elijah gets back. We sent him into town for something; he will be home in about thirty-five minutes. That's just enough time for you gentlemen to freshen up and unpack."

———•———

Lee Ann gently knocked on the guesthouse door. Clay opened it and peered into the gleaming eyes of her smiling face.

"Are you ready?" she quietly asked as if her grandfather would hear her.

The guests said that they were.

"Okay then, follow me."

She led them around the edge of the house to the back porch where Elijah Waters sat, gazing off into the distant sky line. He stood in surprise as Lee Ann turned at the edge of the porch.

"Well, what do we have here?" he said rising to his feet. "I knew you and your Grandmamma were up to something."

His smile was enormous, and his brilliant blue eyes flashed like sparkling water. His complexion was a flawless dark brown, free of wrinkles. He had obviously spent many years below decks away from the sun's punishing rays. His hair was speckled gray and cut low to his head, and his eyebrows were much grayer than his hair. He stood about five feet eight with a lean build and perfectly straight shoulders. He was dressed like a southern gentleman in slacks and a clean, white, button-down shirt, which had perfect creases down the length of each sleeve. He reached up and under his thin leather suspenders, fastened to his light-brown trousers with two buttons each. Hooking his thumbs, he adjusted the suspenders then walked to the edge of the porch in order to greet them.

The deep blue of Elijah's eyes mesmerized Kevin, who searched Elijah's face for the scars from his beating in 1942. Bo had described them in such horrifying detail that the image had stuck hard in his memory. But it looked to Kevin that the scars had faded to the point that just a few fine lines remained, and these were overshadowed by his kind and knowing smile.

"You boys have come a long way to speak to an old man. It must be very important in order for you to set aside part of your summer vacation to spend it with me." Elijah extended his hand and shook Kevin's first and then Leonard's and Clay's as the three of them started up the steps of the back porch.

"This is such a surprise." He laughed, a sound that was pure and rich. "I am sure my granddaughter and wife told you how much I love surprises. Please, have a seat. I knew something was up when Lee Ann and my wife ushered me out of the house, and the smell of those fresh-baked cookies assured me something was going on. Lee Ann told me just a few seconds ago that you were here, but that's all. I understand that you are Bo Kelso's son," he said, looking at Clay.

Clay acknowledged by saying, "Yes sir, that's right."

"Here, everybody have a seat. The best part of the day is about to begin, and this is where I love to spend it. It will be so much better to share it with company. Sit, sit." Elijah stood and waited until everyone was seated before he resumed his seat.

They all settled into cushioned chairs scattered all along the back porch. It overlooked the meticulously maintained lawn all the way down to the Neuse River. Off in the distance, a mockingbird started to sing his cluster of borrowed songs from birds he had encountered, a marvelous melody of short ensembles, rehearsed to perfection. He sang solo in the backyard, entertaining the guests.

"I didn't know there were mockingbirds here," Leonard said.

"Oh yes, just like back home in Texas. His song is different but beautiful nonetheless. I miss the way they sing back in Texas, a repertoire of all the birds they know from their native land. Funny, what this one has learned from other birds, and he uses that to entertain us. Now tell me, why have you boys traveled so far?"

"Mr. Waters," Clay began, "my father started keeping a journal after my mother died in order to soothe his grieving. He gave that journal to these two boys, and they in turn gave it back to me. After reading it, I realized that I had to bring the boys to you, and that I should come too, because I am part of this as well. You see, the journal was kept for you and no one else. It is a template, a rehearsal for the apology he so desperately wanted to give you himself."

Kevin stood and carried the journal to Mr. Waters. As he stood in front of him, Kevin spoke. "This is why we're here, Mr. Waters. We are here to apologize for what Mr. Kelso did to you back in 1942. He has sent Leonard and me together to tell you how truly sorry he is for what happened to you because he can no longer say it himself."

Elijah reached out his hand and removed the book from Kevin's. He opened it to one of the marked pages and began to read. As he did, Leonard and Kevin both started telling Elijah the story of how Bo Kelso had befriended them. As they told their story, he flipped the pages, one after the other, reading to himself and occasionally glancing up to see the vibrant faces of these young boys recounting the wonderful summer they'd spent on Kelso Ranch. They generously offered their memories to Elijah, thereby transferring Bo's kindness to this unimposing black gentleman.

From time to time, there would be tears in Elijah's eyes that he would wipe away with a cotton napkin removed from the tray next to his chair. As the boys spoke, sometimes their words were punctuated with laughter or great drama, depending on the tale. They continued in this way for almost an hour before the conversation was exhausted and it was Elijah's turn to speak.

Elijah had listened closely to the boys as they so effortlessly recounted their story to him. He knew why the two of them had been sent to him by Mr. Beauregard Lee Kelso—they were his masterpiece. The two of them were a genuine expression of the things Bo had learned in his living. There was no purer confession of truth than the two of them together telling their story.

In the boys' genuine words and expressions, Elijah could see that they were not raised with hatred, cruelty, or prejudice. A link in a chain that was over two hundred years old had been broken. And he knew that these boys would not teach their children the stupidity and ignorance of past generations, who carelessly, through small words and deeds, had passed on seeds of such hatred.

"I am so proud of the three of you, and more importantly, I'm extremely proud of your parents. They did not teach you that people should be divided in one way or another. They obviously taught you to be kind and understanding to all those around you. The three of you will do the same to your children and those children will be inclined to do the same for their children. It is this simple thing, passed down from one generation to the next, that will make this world a better place for everyone.

"I hold no grudge against Beauregard Lee Kelso. I forgave him a long time ago for what happened to me. I moved on and made a better life for myself. It wasn't Beauregard's fault; he'd only done what he thought was right. He did not have the opportunity to grow up the way the three of you did. His thoughts were crushed between the anvil of prejudice and the hammer of hatred. Those are two very powerful factors for a young impressionable boy to overcome. He did the best he could.

"You see, the truth is, boys, that there is nothing for me to forgive. I was determined not to be defined by what happened or to let it suffocate me. If I had allowed that, it would have stopped me from being a better man each day and finding a better life each day. I didn't carry around the anger in my heart, and I have had my share of prejudice and hatred directed at me. I've been a cook on a ship full of nothing but white men during World War II. I saw prejudice three times a day and in every hallway and passageway. However, all along the way I also met people like the three of you, and they were the remedy that kept my spirits up all my life. I'm not sure you young boys see the big picture here, but Beauregard did, and that's why you're here. No offense to you, Mr. Clay. I'm sure you understood what a fine man your father had become, but the two of you," Elijah said, stretching out his large hand and pointing to the two boys one by one, "are the most important part of this equation."

The two boys turned toward one another and looked into each other's faces with wide eyes, curious as to these last words Elijah spoke.

"You see, words scribbled into a book cannot convey true emotion," the elderly man said. "They are simply pieces of things arranged to make a sound. That sound has a meaning that must be translated. However, when words come from the mouth of someone who has lived those words, they mean much more. They have true value. The two of you are a testimony straight from the heart of Beauregard Kelso. The fact that he sent you to me proves that he is a good man and has lived a good, right, and full life. When I look into your eyes, I see the childhood Beauregard never had, and most importantly, I see how big his heart is. The three of you are a gift from him to me."

A comfortable silence settled over the conversation as the three of them pondered the words of one who seemed so much bigger and wiser than themselves, someone who was able to connect the generations and their meanings.

Elijah leaned back in his chair and opened Bo's journal to the page that began with this sentence, "*Never have I seen such a rain, and I'm sure there has never been such a flood, a flood that unveiled the prejudice and arrogance I so blindly ignored.*

"Boys, now you must pass that gift on to everyone you meet and, more importantly, to your children. Just like the mockingbird singing in the trees on both our shores, the song you teach your children is the song they will sing."

# 37

"Uncle Clint!" Mary Beth shouted as she leaned over backward against the weight of the huge fish that devoured her bait. "I got a big one!"

Clint lifted the brim of his hat just high enough over his forehead to gaze up from his sitting position in the large folding beach chair. Mary Beth's big brother and two cousins ran over to assist her. The fish was massive and leaped into the air, as if to show off his impressive size. By the time it had splashed back into the water, Mary Beth had a full audience with all the Kelso grandchildren cheering her on. The girl was only seven years, the latest and perhaps the last addition to Clay's family—a new sprig on a family tree steeped in tradition and legacy.

The fish jumped again, then again. With each acrobatic display, the five children, who ranged in ages from fifteen down to Mary Beth's seven, screamed with excitement.

Uncle Clint, as he was now called—an endearment that the children had bestowed upon him some years back—tried his best to force his eyes back down and return to his blissful nap. The shade of the trees along the old sand mine was like a rocking cradle for the soul as drowsiness pulled Clint in.

The crystal waters of the lake had became a favorite haven for the family since the boys, Kevin and Leonard, rediscovered it. Clay and Jeb hired someone to clear the road so it would be more easily accessible by truck. Meanwhile, Clint's title had grown from keeper of the barn to glorified babysitter of the

Kelso grandchildren two days a week during the summer—on top of his usual duties.

Bo Kelso had made sure that Clint was well taken care of and gave him lifetime rights to the ranch house as long as he wanted to stay. It not only was Bo's wish, but that of his wife's as well. Kevin and Leonard fished the pond almost every weekend and worked in the barn up to the day both of them left for college at Texas A&M. Leonard and his mother Lynette had pushed Kevin past what he thought to be his academic limits in order to bolster his GPA so he could attend college with his best friend. It was what Bo would have wanted, especially as he'd left both their families a trust fund, set up by his sons' law firm, in order for the two of them to achieve a degree.

"Uncle Clint, you got to help us," Clay's oldest son, Jeb Jr., said.

Not because he really needed the help, Clint knew. He just wanted to involve old Clint in what was turning out to be a family affair. Clint smiled and sat up in his chair. He pushed his hat all the way back on his head as he pulled his legs up so he could stand from the low-sitting beach chair.

"Okay, give me just a minute, but I don't see what good I'll be. There are enough of you down there to hoist up a whale."

The children all laughed hysterically as the reel started to scream and relinquish the line to the powerful fish. Just then, from behind Clint, Whisky appeared and walked past.

"Where are you going?"

Whisky ignored Clint as he headed toward the cool clear water full of splashing children. He even flipped his tail as he passed Clint. The long, thick, broom-like hairs struck Clint on the side of his face and knocked off his black Stetson hat. It landed on the ground directly in front of him.

"All right now. Don't forget, I have your apple, and as smart as you are, you still can't open a saddlebag."

Whisky stopped and craned his head around to meet Clint's eyes. *The look.* The beautiful horse waited for Clint to come alongside him and gently pressed his muzzle against Clint's neck. Clint dusted off his hat before returning it to its perch atop his head.

"Oh, I ain't mad at you. No need for that," Clint said, reaching up to give Whisky a gentle pat on his neck.

These were Clint's favorite days during the summer, especially since the boys had moved on in pursuit of life. He thoroughly enjoyed riding Whisky to the lake with young Mary Beth sitting in front, holding the reins and giggling. Funny how the laughter of a child could soothe the pain of an old injury, enabling the ache in his knee to abate long enough so he could enjoy a slow walk to treasured places.

At the end of the day, Clay, Jeb, or one of their wives would drive to the farmhouse and retrieve all the children. They were always dirty, covered in grass, hay, or trail dust. Some days they all would be soaking wet to the point that their parents insisted they changed their clothes before entering the vehicle. On this particular day, Clay had arrived early to retrieve the rambunctious troop.

"Daddy! Daddy! Look at the fish," Mary Beth squealed.

Her shrieks were powerful and shrill enough to break glass each time the massive bass broke water and launched into the air. Clay had no idea what was going on until Jeb pointed and explained in quick fashion that his youngest sister was hanging onto a monster at the end of her fishing line. By the time Clay walked over to the edge of the lake, Clint had taken up position next to Whisky at the water's edge.

"What is going on?" Clay questioned.

"Your daughter has hooked what appears to be the biggest fish in the lake and is putting up a good fight with no help. The other kids tried to take over the rod, but she fought them off as hard as she is fighting that fish."

The bass made one more massive jump straight into the

air. It violently shook its head and seemed to hover like a hummingbird just for a split second, and in that brief fraction of time, everyone witnessed the magnificence of the fish. They all gasped in unison, then as suddenly as it appeared, it was gone. Down, down, deep it dove, shredding off line from the reel, descending to the deepest part of the lake. Suddenly the fight was over. The monster was not fighting anymore. The line was still tight, though it was not dancing or jerking. Something was holding it tight, heavy and still at the bottom of the lake.

"Oh no, Daddy, help. It's stuck." Mary Beth pulled up the tip of the rod, and it went slack. She began to cry. Clay waded into the water in his loafers and dress slacks up to his ankles and picked her up. Her wet shorts soaked the front of his white, long-sleeve shirt as he shifted her around in his arms. She dropped the fishing pole into the twelve-inch deep water and hugged her father's neck, sobbing so that her tears soaked the back of his shirt. He did his best to console her, reminding her that she would catch an even bigger fish next time.

"Are you sure?" she asked, still hanging tightly to his neck and gasping between sobs.

"Of course I'm sure. You know why?"

"Why?"

Clay bent down and reached into the water, picking up the rod and reel. The water drained from the reel like dripping tears as he walked back to the shoreline with Mary Beth in his arms. Whatever was hung onto the end was being drug across the bottom of the lake until he reached the shore and placed Mary Beth on the sandy beach.

"Because we'll come back until you do. Now here. You go and pull in whatever it is, and we'll start over again."

Mary Beth tried as hard as she could to pull the mystery ashore, but it was just too heavy for her little frame. Clay took the rod from her hands and reeled a little, then pulled a little, reeled a little, pulled a little, until the thing emerged from the bottom in a muddy clump. Jeb Jr. picked up the line and followed it down into the water waist-high. Reaching down with his hands, he lifted what appeared at first to be a limb as big around as a man's arm and twice as long. They brought it to Clay. Mary Beth's face wrinkled up in disgust at the gooey hunk of mud, which emitted an odiferous odor like sulfur.

"Ew, Daddy. Get it away," Mary Beth said as her father removed the hook from the clump of stinky mud. Having lost interest, she returned to the other children near the water.

Clint stood motionless as if he had seen a ghost, one that he thought would never return to haunt him again. Clay bent down in the water to rinse the mud from the object, squeezing and pulling and splashing until it took on an unmistakable form—an old single-barrel shotgun.

"How about that?" Clay examined the rusted relic. "How do you suppose that got out there?"

"It got out there because that's where it belongs," Clint said, heading back to his shade and beach chair. Clay followed him, still clutching the old shotgun, dripping muddy water out of the barrel.

Clint eased his body down into his beach chair and drew in a long, deep breath. In the far distance the church bells, in the new steeple of the Clover Town Pentecostal Church, marked the passing of another hour. Clay leaned against the truck just a few feet from Clint, waiting for the explanation he assumed he was sure Clint had.

"You see, some years ago that shotgun conspired with a bottle of whisky and tried to convince me that my life would be a whole lot better if I wasn't living it," Clint admitted. "I almost gave in to the seduction of cold steel and the hypnotic dance of bubbles as they fell from the end of a bottle and tangled up my thoughts. The drink and the barrel offered me the comfort I was so desperately searching for. One was quicker than the other, and to me they both were fighting each other to see who would get me first. I was a miserable sort, wretched and unhappy to the point of letting them have me, but something, or someone, changed me."

Clint paused and looked in the direction of the children casting their lines standing in clear, knee-deep water. Three of them stood on the left of Whisky and two to his right—a horse that was so much more than just an animal He was one of the family who loved to entertain and be entertained. His favorite place seemed to be close to the children, as close as he could possibly get whenever they were around.

"I swear if that horse could cast a rod and reel he would fish all day with those kids," Clay remarked as he sensed a break in their conversation.

"He can do more than that. He can talk," Clint said.

Clay looked at him waiting for the punch line. "Talk?"

"Yep, that horse along with his momma stopped me from using that shotgun one morning. He convinced me that I should reconsider my horrible idea and wait for divine guidance."

Not sure what Clint was going to say next, Clay was nonetheless intrigued and stayed silent, waiting for him to continue.

"Your mother fell from the heavens and saw right through me. Her sweet, blue eyes penetrated my thoughts and pulled the pain from my heart, like poison from a festering wound. She told me, 'Don't let the weeds have it.'"

Clay immediately recognized his mother's favorite metaphor about the garden. His eyes moistened as he recalled the power behind that woman's simple words when it came to solving even the most tangled problems. From a splinter in his own small finger as a child to his first broken heart, Clay remembered how her soothing words repaired everything and left no lingering scar.

"That rusted heap of metal you hold in your hands represents agony and all that was wrong in my life—it along with a whisky bottle, which also lies at the bottom of the lake,"

Clint said, knowing why they were put there, and who had done the putting. "Both belong there and should stay there. Some things just need to stay at the bottom of a lake."

Clay shook his head as he looked up from the rusted shotgun into Clint's squinting eyes, which were clear, brilliant, and full of hope. The eyes of a believer.

Walking to the edge of the lake, Clay paused for just a moment before entering the water waist-high, where with a mighty heave, he flung the shotgun into the deepest part of the lake.

And the only "whisky" found anywhere on the property slept in the cleanest barn in Texas.